THE
VALLEY
a void

THE
VALLEY
a void

Vanessa Roveto

SPBH & ITI Novellas No. 1

The giant artificial palm tree that anchors the luxury condos off Ventura Boulevard bursts into flames. Burning fronds send smoke signals upward, engulfing a helicopter in bong-ripped plumes. Blades chop through the dark-lung air. At a nearby restaurant, Reality TV celebrities in summer-wear plunge forks into raw kale and idly watch the complex catch fire. In the back alley of the restaurant, by the sewers, hungry street rats chew each other to death. Westward down the boulevard closer to the Pacific shore, a pelican swallows beach glass. Ocean salt gathers itself into pyramids, preparing for a resurrection. Time dilates as the Santa Anas swipe living palm trees, bending the trunks toward the pleated grounds of manicured grass. Bored and still feeling the effects of sleeping pills, you slowly crane your neck upward toward a strange visual. A car is suspended in the air, flying off the cliffs of Mulholland Drive.

VICTORIA

I have this recurring dream.

MADELINE

last night i ate cold cereal and listened to badly drawn boy's first album on repeat and went to sleep at 5 am. at 3 pm i woke up in a dreadful mood.

after taking a shower for what seemed like half a day, i picked up my corpse, put on my darkest sunglasses and my gg allin "legalize murder" shirt, went to the diner on moorpark and installed myself in a corner booth. i ordered pancakes that i didn't eat and several cups of coffee all of which i drank and stared at the wood paneling, trying to imagine a different life. i thought about this one time in 11th grade when these mean girls asked why i was dressed like a lesbian camp counselor and my knee socks were supposed to be like a french school girl look so i really felt like shit. and my twin brother guillaume who we all call guy because he is rightly embarrassed by the name drove us up to the top of mulholland to smoke weed and listen to guns n roses "don't you cry" on repeat. guy told me i needed to be like the model stephanie seymour in that music video where she's at a bar and a rival chick comes over and she bitch slaps her. he told me, "don't cry. act like a fucking supermodel." thinking of that, i began crying unlike a supermodel into a handful of cheap one-ply paper napkins. turns out, pharmaceutical drugs are not the answer to everything.

VICTORIA

I started having weird visualizations as a teenager. I made films in my head out of all kinds of things: a feeling, a cooked-shrimp ring, smog. Really compelling shit. But sometimes these films got mixed into reality, so I couldn't tell if I was in them or watching them. Eventually, I found space for it all in my head, for both of these perspectives, both of me. And I lived it over and over again.

*

My ex, Dora, used to say I was impenetrable, a "mysterious lesbian." I thought maybe she said this because of my heavy brow, my starvation rituals, my semi-permanent scowl, my weird animalistic sexuality, a gay Marlon Brando in *Mutiny on the Bounty*.

I dumbly thought Love could save "mysterious," but later I realized weirdos are typically left to their own devices. I was no exception but rather part of a long, honored tradition of mangled people who are too broken to fake it.

In *Mutiny on the Bounty*, Brando's lover offers him words of Tahitian wisdom: "Tahiti people say, 'You eat life, or life eat you.'"

Life is a film that never quite turns out like the trailer made you think it would. On the blurred edges of your vision is a playground, a feral dog chewing a chocolate wrapper, a couple of queer teenagers doing poppers, someone's grandpa sloping in the sun over a Corona. Basketball nets swish, followed by demonic cheering. You're stuck in a broken lawn chair, trapped because you don't know how to get out of something.

I know that people either find my eccentric behavior extremely annoying or incredibly endearing and that there isn't really much gray area. I know that people who find me annoying generally dislike me with ease and can't stand to be around me, so I find myself surrounded by people who enjoy my weirdness and therefore I never really get a lot of constructive criticism except for the voices in my head.

For this reason, I became a poet. At 42, I teach in Last Chance, Iowa. To my students, I am a beast of burden, a lone mule across a fence that separates me from others and their experiences, a cross-eyed and unpopular type who is a lesbian not because of any innate sexual preference but rather because I scared all the men away with my animal moaning sounds. In any case, that's what one of my student evaluations said.

✻

Today I lead my students in a writing exercise. I tell them to go outside and for two minutes straight write down everything they observe, then for the next two minutes write down everything they think and then compare the two, a lesson in subjectivity, memory, note-taking.

So we all go outside and take part in the prompt. I write down for two minutes: *pigeons, single smashed french fry, succulents with sun damage, my own aging hands, a pale eminem face in aztec banana king diamond shirt (euro tour) white belt dad style cutoff jean shorts black socks all white suede vans rosie o'donnell haircut.* I write for two minutes more: *If I was standing in this poem would I be wearing a hazmat suit and would the*

*poem change if I took a bong rip and on the way down
I grab a cloud, the clown, or another cosmic prosthesis
that reminds you of your father?*

One of my favorite students, Aron, a five-foot-three
Turkish poet, writes: *birds; no birds.*

✳

These days the only time I feel less lonely is in the company of other lonely poets: deeply nerdy, damaged people
who were poorly socialized as children, with tattoos of
their narcissistic injuries. We eat Chinese food awkwardly
with chopsticks, poking at fungus and water chestnuts,
trying to gain insight into the disarray of our own lives
and that of the fungi, where we're going and where we've
been, describing the world in detail as a way to get closer
to it, a loner's existence crystallized in the chili oil-stained
paper menu. The life we required for art was a life without animate companions. I'd eat dumplings forever with
them if I could.

✳

Hm, Iowa. What is there to say? If someone were to ask
(no one ever does) I would tell them that, for me, Iowa
is a soothing maternal bosom, calming, whereas my
hometown—The Valley adjacent Los Angeles—is a dry-
milk-duct hell, where I easily become unpredictable and
mad. I would tell them about the charming food and local
characters in Iowa, especially a homeless person known
as Dr. Nicky, who wanders downtown at night, accosting people on the pedestrian mall, warning everyone he
meets or who will listen that women are ruled by the moon,
their periods synced with the tides, and to counsel the

constellations before going near the fairer sex but above all to distrust them. Dr. Nicky previously worked at the Emma Goldman Clinic for women and revolutionaries. He was the town's foremost gynecologist.

I haven't seen Dr. Nicky since last summer, when he left the local winter shelter, which he had confused for his old office, decorating it with dusty forceps and a female anatomy skeleton. He told me how he had hand-carved *MD* into the door. Then excitedly he took out of his pocket a printout of a photo of a farm chicken and her three chicks. He told me these were the last babies he had delivered. On the image, there were hearts drawn in ink and the words, "My eternal thanks to the good doctor!!"

I once asked Dr. Nicky what he thought about my "nervous breakdowns." He told me that medically speaking, there is no such thing. It's just a fancy way of saying, "You're nuts." He also said to take extra Xanax *before* I freak out and to listen to Sid Vicious.

✶

My twin brother, Will, used to love Sid Vicious. As teens, we tried to start a punk band called Aquapuke. It was supposed to be about excess and taking the extravagances of the rock and roll lifestyle to the extreme, particularly in regard to partying until puking. I even wrote out a script for a potential video, where we were wandering around North Hollywood, going from house party to house party, and vomiting non-stop in the swimming pools. Revolution, hurrrl style. In any case, we both got sent to the "happy house," so Aquapuke was short-lived.

MADELINE

i am 19 years old, i am (temporarily, fakely) blonde, and i live in the san fernando valley in a tract home. my father divorced my mom a few years ago and moved to the castro in san fran (more on why another time) and is a personal shopper for men (this is a clue). my mother, celine, has an artistic background and won some notoriety for a painting of julia child being attacked by chicken legs. she turned that into a career as a home scenic designer, which means she paints murals of magical things onto the walls of the homes of wealthy people.

she went a bit insane when my father left us, notably drawing feces all over the paintings in our house, signing them all "motherwell." sometimes she dates men who we meet, sometimes she dates men who she only meets in her mind.

she named me madeline as in that annoying french child with tuberculosis. everyone calls me 'mad' as in the feeling or circumstance, as in anger or insanity.

i dropped out of college and moved back home after i stopped eating when my dad left us and became fully gay (no kidding), a hunger strike of sorts. i work part-time at whole foods and spend the rest of the time thinking my "little important thoughts," as my mother likes to call them.

i also live with my two siblings. my twin brother guy i've already mentioned, the one who told me to bitch slap my bully in 11th grade. we were much closer then, even more so when we were little, concocting two-person-only games and writing the occasional duet for air guitar. these days he's rather passionate and likes to go on knowledge rants such as how "the ancients knew that whole milk was superior to skim milk." sometimes his passion overtakes him and he starts throwing stuff around and breaking things (which in a young woman might be sexy but in a young man is somewhat excessive). last night for example he lost a game of scrabble and subsequently kicked over the table. he then went into a rant about feminism and the family dog, sara: "sara is the sister i've never had!" i think he was joking but it hurt, especially because we aren't so close anymore.

then there's my abnormally tall and abnormally theatrical sister jewel (known as "broadway baby" by guy and me), about to turn 16 and officially ruin all our lives. jewel has an overly performative way of speaking, as though every person is an audience or, better yet, a casting agent. this happens even in casual conversation at home. just asking what's for dinner becomes her cabaret. my mother had her at 44, and sometimes i wonder if jewel's innate issues might be attributed to the geriatric pregnancy or an ivf snafu.

my parents named her jewel because our recently estranged father loves gaudy things and my mom loves the painter john waterhouse. her favorite of his is a painting of a tall, slim brunette woman holding a large crystal ball. i heard that when the painting was restored not too long ago it revealed a human skull sitting near the figure that a previous owner had painted over. i think the revealed skull adds a touch of symbolism to the entire family affair.

jewel is an alien to me: overly upbeat, with the energy of a jumping worm. it's very odd in contrast to guy and me and our inborn inclination toward foreign film and lying in bed all day. guy is the only person who truly understands my morbidity.

a few years ago when i was feeling especially self-absorbed and pompously miserable he insisted my mom adopt a rabbit for me from the rabbit rescue activists who used to visit the pet store on colfax. he named it stephanie after stephanie seymour, who he always said i looked like, which wasn't true but was a massive compliment. it turned out stephanie was actually a boy and had a fatal disease that rendered him nonexistent only 6 months after we got him. we buried him out back behind the house alongside jewel's hamster named cheetah, who escaped her cage and got crushed by the trash compactor. guy gave a very moving speech where he pretended to be jean-luc godard, which mostly entailed him speaking in a bad french accent. for some reason, i actually cried at the funeral, my first (funeral, not cry). guy saw how upset i was and started singing "for she was a jolly good fellow." i started laughing but kept crying, probably not for stephanie but because our dad had just left. guy held my hand the entire time. i miss that version of him.

VICTORIA

It's evening (4 am), so I work myself into an obituary:

Victoria Blank, poetry professor and writer of several unpopular books of poetry and prose—notably Oedipus Complex and Electra Complex, about two crumbling apartment complexes breaking down in tandem with family structures—passed away at middle age.

The cause was brain failure, said her mother Skyla, 70, an art historian with a fairy fetish, who had died some years before.

Reared in the San Fernando Valley, she was born an only child but was joined moments later by a sibling, both of them born the same day, the season of Gemini. "The Gemini personality is either something or nothing," Victoria was once quoted as saying in her own head. "One day I tried doing nothing for a week in the middle of the Pacific. My mind turned to pharmaceutical interventions." The twins were followed by a theatrical but forgettable sibling, Crystal, who walked with the kind of delusional self-assurance of a woman who has never achieved anything significant in her life.

Victoria was the type of woman who could only be believed when she was being most unbelievable, a mirror held up to another mirror in the dreams of others. She would complain of the wind blowing through her hair, giving her a bad hair day, but there was no wind. Her weathervane was inside, shifting depending on which phantom she was speaking to. Which mood or dimension

would overtake her, ordering the meaningless days?
She could hardly guess. Boo hoo.

I read this out loud and suddenly remember: I forgot
to take my antidepressant this morning!

✳

My biological father named me after Vincente Minelli.
Victoria was the closest female name he could come up
with. Theatrical, Italian, and, later, homosexual, much
like Vincente, my father gave me a lot to work with and
through. His eyes would well up with tears over a single
perfect spaghetti strand, yet his ducts would go dry when
confronted with a child's booboo. He was hairless. His
breasts, no bigger than baby's fists, were always, somehow, exposed.

My father didn't come from money, nor did he move
toward money, unless it was someone else's. He did, however, teach me how to make the most of a can of Italian
tuna, how to get dinner for free (find your own hair in the
eggplant parm), how to shoplift VHS gay porn. For my
16th birthday, he stole an erotic lesbian calendar from
Le Sex Shoppe and made me open the gift at Pinocchio's
Restaurant. I remember the embarrassment gnawing
away at me as he grabbed and waved the gift, shouting to
the perplexed patrons, "So proud of my GAY daughter!"

Later, during the quiet ride home from dinner, a free
eggplant parm in my lap, he asked with genuine curiosity, "Why don't you ever celebrate *me*?"

✳

Honestly, my father's theatrics would often amuse me,
the way he lorded over his small amount of knowledge

with a great sense of pride and verve. "I'm the original feminist in this family! I read *Italian Vogue*! I've seen all of Barbra Streisand's films *at least* twice!" he would say, just before leveling an insult about my weak smile. Each time it was a little different, but somehow I was always moved in one way or another by this character he was playing. I was absorbed in his self-absorption, absorbed by a princess who liked to strut his stuff. He's not entirely unlike his estranged child Crystal. We're all an audience to their one-woman shows.

＊

Much to my father's working-class disappointment and that of all the gendered ancestors, the descendants of sausage-making peasants back in the old country, I got my MFA in poetry. My thesis was, naturally, all about him: a poem inspired by Marguerite Duras, David Lynch, Lily Tomlin, PTSD, Monica's Vitti's face in *Red Desert*, stimulants and cookies, years alone at sea, aids, Artaud, shoulder pads, lesbian psychosis, pricked balloons and entropy, cells unwinding in the blood.

But I've soured on ambition. I'm all for humility, a monk essentially. Sorry, I meant drunk. So I throw myself nightly into a bottle of Everclear with a chaser of mashed pills. On a good evening, I'll write a few perfectly polished sentences in the voice of my father:

I was Elizabeth Taylor. Now I have no friends. I belch I fart I am the unstoppable star and I am star

＊

Sometimes I dream of my father and I meeting, each bringing a piece of paper with an inventory of the things we wish we could say out loud to one another.

"I'll begin," my father says:
    1. I wanted to see the world.

Then a long period of silence. He finally says he tried to make a larger inventory, but then showed it to a friend who helped him boil it down to its essence.

I read mine back to him:
    1. It's okay. I forgive you.
    2. On more than one occasion, I stole money out of your pants to buy toys you wouldn't get me. One of those toys was a doll I called "Bad Daddy." She was my favorite doll.

All the Valley dwellers have become sensitive. You join them and become a prepper, too. You've gone from "as if" to "what if." Instability brings about everyone's rampaging for jarred capers, electrolytes, boxes of instant cranberry bread. Bearing long biblical beards and thinness, you're all suddenly radical as fuck, yelling out improvised poems from cars, developing personal slogans that all amount to Bereft of Life. Against cloudless skies, any of the available disorders are at your disposal. The desert air crisps up the context.

MADELINE

my second-floor bedroom window looks out onto a parched, dust-bowl landscape the color of that brown m&m that was discontinued, and this is why i think of nothing but death.

to the left of the window frame are the sad fronds of an aging palm tree. in the distance, another luxury building and another. there is the occasional noisy visitation from a parrot (something about a pet store that caught fire in van nuys and animals escaping and procreating).

the woman who cleans our house, marina, keeps 17 birds in her apartment in cages. last week she showed me a picture of a bird she calls "snow." snow is a syphilitic cockatiel who has pink eye, an addiction to twizzlers, and a flesh wound on her neck from self-abuse. if that isn't a metaphor!

i just caught my reflection in the framed poster of *the gospel according to st. matthew* on my bedroom wall and jesus i look like a miserable horrible person, not having showered or eaten in days. i was up until 5am impulse-buying myriad things, not least of which was a david lynch print of a photograph of a rotting clay head partly made of lunch meat neatly titled "clay head with turkey, cheese and ants," which made me hungry (afterward i took a single slice of soy cheese from the fridge into bed). but hey, at least i'm not my twin, who spent all dinner ranting about an art opening he went to in shipping containers near skid row. guy complained about hipsters drinking microbrews and talking about the yugoslav new wave and admiring art made out of trash, while people were living in literal trash on the streets nearby. i guess we're both feeling more than a bit debased these days.

i've been spending an inordinate amount of time inside my room because people are very, very tiring. just today i heard from the internet that harvard is handing out a phd in critical fierceness to a gay-male artist/dj in their midst. um a "doctor" in fierceness? rome is falling, big time. just kill me now. (btw a total case of discrimination here. if this were a lesbian, she'd be laughed straight out of the ivy league and back to her job at juicy couture.)

anyway, i've been lying in bed avoiding "the adults" in the house, my brother and my mother, listening to pink floyd feeling sad and angry with myself that i wasn't working on anything creative. the "two lost souls swimming in a fish bowl" lyric is an especially embarrassingly accurate description of my fractured, guppyfied, expanding-waistline self.

guy is super-creative. he could turn a piece of driftwood into a sculpture some palm springs homosexuals would pay money for to display on their turquoise mantelpiece (this actually happened). jewel aspires to be an artist and certainly has a knack for improvised everyday performance but somehow doesn't inspire me. to be fair, it isn't her job to do so. she just has an uncanny ability to make me feel more alien in my own body. i look at her and see my nose, my eye color, freckles, but i can't quite find a connection.

i wish i could commiserate with guy about jewel, but he hasn't been the same since our father left our mother a while back for a man named gayle, which all things being equal, is a pretty great name for a homo. guy and i were best friends up until the age of 13 or so, when we both developed daddy issues. driven by self-loathing, he started smashing things and i started reading nietzsche.

this is all just a long-winded way of saying i've just actually been feeling really far away from "who i am" (putting these words in quotes makes me feel less like an asshole) and feeling at great risk of settling into a dull life of mediocrity. i am loathe to admit this but i've just been feeling like, insofar as i have any, i'm not taking full advantage of my creative "potential" by getting better. i have also been worried that, even if i should finally take advantage, i might find that i have absolutely nothing to offer! that in fact there's no there-there, no "voice," and that ultimately i'm a fairly dull, passionless person. it's a pretty awful feeling. also i know it sounds kind of psychotic (literally) calling it a "voice," but it's the best i can come up with.

having said that i do give myself credit for clawing my way out of my own particular primordial sludge to become a more relatively functional person. but sometimes i wish i was just extraordinary and not "extraordinary, all things considered." i feel very embarrassed, having just written that, especially since no one has ever used that exact word, "extraordinary," to describe me, but i guess i do, sort of in the back of my mind, want to be exceptional in one way or another. guess that's human frailty for you.

i wish i could talk to guy about all this. i get so sad about us not being able to commiserate. in vain, i emailed him (although he was just in the other room):

jewel was especially amusing today. i wanted to tell you about it. i guess i'm sick of pretending like you not being in my life doesn't hurt... because it does. i just really miss you.

he never responded.

when i told our mother what i wrote and asked if she thought it was a bad idea for me to have done it she said: "whatever floats your boat." it was perhaps the most singularly hilarious and emotionally maladjusted example of bad parenting i've ever experienced. i don't think it could be improved upon.

VICTORIA

This morning starts like any other in the Midwest. I take my coffee in the solarium. I pick at a piece of bone-dry toast. I listen to my neighbor's obese chicken Henrietta cluck as she lays her daily egg. I read my students' poems in such microscopic detail that I suffer temporary blindness and walk into the wall.

Aron turns in a poem that engages with ideas about attachment and exhibitionism, where the subject meets the object, where the speaker inserts a pair of dazzling diamond-encrusted teeth rectally. It seemed like a difficult way to make a statement about vanity and speech, and led to a free-wheeling discussion about fetishism, fascism, and dentistry. As the teeth are one of the final things to go, you can still identify a corpse by its teeth, especially if they are bedazzled. And I saw for an instant my own elegy in this poem's piece of paper blowing through space and time, birdlike hieroglyphic origami, diving straight to my Valley childhood and into the Ventura freeway's meridian.

I check the weather: -30F with wind chill, cold enough to sober me up. I put on my Arctic parka, my gloves, my boots, my face-mask, my UV-blocking glasses, my ice traction cleats. I open the door and the wind smacks me. It takes me several minutes to make it ten steps to my mailbox, which is shaped like a woodpecker with a mohawk. I reach my gloved hand in and paw at the one letter inside.

A black-hooded parka likely containing a person floats in front of the mailbox, and like a shell without a spirit, seems to disappear into the mist. Probably a grad student of mine.

Back at my desk, I look at my letter, which has my mother's return address on it. Inside is a photograph of my brother Will as a teenager, back when he was dropping a lot of acid, with our father at a dude ranch. My father took him to Wyoming to explore masculinity. In the photo, my brother's holding a lasso like it's dental floss and, in his other hand, a lit cigarette, looking more like Camus than John Wayne. My father is wearing an ascot. It's a very strange Western.

I finger the photo's tattered edges, its blurs, its coffee-stained corner. I feel my body moving away from me.

I put the photo down and pick up the letter, staring at my mother's handwriting, which begins: "hi honey. i don't know how to say this. they're gone." My dad left decades ago, so she must mean Will. My eyes blur as I read on.

Something about his car going straight off a cliff.

✳

Time takes off and so do I.

I ask the university for a period of mourning to attend my brother's funeral. "He killed himself. Auto-erotica. Boom!" I gesture wildly to the other poetry faculty. Then I pop an Adderall under my tongue, pull *Mrs. Dalloway* from my pocket, and read an especially suicidal passage:

> Death was defiance. Death was an attempt to communicate; people feeling the impossibility of reaching

the centre, which, mystically, evaded them; closeness drew apart; rapture faded, one was alone.

"I underlined the word *alone*," I tell them. No one says a word, so I remind my audience that bipolar Spike Milligan's gravestone epigraph is "I told you I was ill!" Then I take off my Ray-Bans and stare at everyone, and run outside, hopping into my vintage Honda. I turn on the car and gas it straight into a snowdrift, which deploys the airbag straight into my face.

Recovering in bed, I text Crystal, *how you holding up?* She responds, *devastated*. I experience a moment of hope, that I'll reconnect or perhaps connect for the first time with my estranged sister to survive this tragedy, and that we'll get through it together. Crystal sends another text, *I was rejected from the Royal Tampa Academy of Dramatic Tricks! When it rains, it pours!*

When my collarbone feels better, I hit the road for the Valley: never more alone.

MADELINE

i'm sitting at the dinner table alone dipping tofu on spikes into peanut sauce, the most civilized thing that's ever happened at this table.

when my dad and mom were still together they used to have elaborate dinner parties where everyone would go on and on about how they'd failed to live up to the delusional optimism of their youth. one of them would typically say to another, "how did i become my own mother?" to which another would reply, "i can't name a single rapper anymore!" and later "my wig flew, my acne popped, my spine slipped, my heart almost gave up, but hey it was a great workout!"

this self-flagellation ritual went on for hours and hours as they picked around food that didn't meet the standards of their eating disorders. they talked endlessly about their problems like they were outside of their control, like an asteroid or the death of a celebrity's kid. it only ended when jewel ran into the room screaming, saying she couldn't feel her legs (even though her legs worked well enough that she was able to run in to tell everyone this). i wasn't especially sympathetic and went up to my room to read *notes from the underground* as i had my own little "notes" to write. the "adults" meanwhile made guy call 911 and the emt gave jewel a prescription for benzos. guy got jewel a best actress trophy for her performance. jewel displayed it next to her participation trophy for taking part in a childhood diabetes fundraiser. she wasn't diabetic, but wanted to feel like she was part of something.

VICTORIA

I keep squinting at this very tiny, dwarf photograph of my brother, now sitting on the dashboard of my car, with Last Chance behind me and in the foreground my Valley childhood, the whispering palms, the Santa Anas blowing dust and death, desert ashes. Why bother being born at all if you have to face the horrors of living all by yourself? Instead of a therapist, I need a wife. Or a nurse practitioner.

*

That first night back in the Valley, I wander into buildings—a pharmacy, a hotel lobby, a dog hospital, hoping to make a connection. My gaze hits the reflective surface of a tin of Iams chunky dog food, the brand that killed my childhood dog. In the class-action lawsuit, my family was awarded thirteen dollars. Will, the closest human to her, never got over her death.

I stare at the Idle Hour, the last standing barrel-shaped bar and the last standing barrel-shaped building in the Valley, a barrel of laughs, a casket barreling toward obsolescence. It faces the San Gabriel Mountains, a range that knows a thing or two about permanence and impermanence, as it seeds itself only to consistently catch fire, up in smoke, distress-signaling. I'm in my own distress, signaling nothing.

Being my father's daughter, I wander into the Beverly Garland Hotel for a free breakfast. Over the fake fireplace, I find a framed candid black-and-white photograph of Beverly sitting casually on a chaise lounge, being herself, whoever that was. There's a handwritten quote underneath: "Stand porter to your mind." I stare and blur my vision until the "I" fractures into a collage of desires amassing into a "Me"—me resent daddy, me hate to wait, me want a muffin.

✳

William tried to warn me about his death. Last Boxing Day, a Canadian holiday my brother believed had a pugnacious spirit, Will was off his meds and he wrote me this:

Heads up V this is truly rare! I don't know anybody who is having a 1 in 20 year conjunction like this happening right on a natal point. The fixed quality of Aquarius (your moon) will further cement your goal in time and space. Whatever commences will endure.

I lied:

this is very helpful william!

I continued:

been trying to have a highly intentioned morning wrote within the 9:00 hour, then test drove cars i can't afford and ate pizza crusts discarded by a friend. i hope i'm living my life correctly but who can ever tell

He said:

I've been seeing how fast I can go. This isn't a metaphor. My buddy and I souped up a Subaru WRX and I've been speeding the entirety of Mulholland Drive, which is about 20 miles. Today's record was 9.25 minutes. But I beat it every day. Right now it's the only thing that makes me feel alive.

The next month—March 21, 2021, the first day of Spring—William was dead.

✳

I try to sleep, but William is standing in front of me: ghostly pale, effeminate, with black hair and a dim, far-away look in his eyes.

"Marx was suicidal, too," he whispers.

I whisper back: "Any philosophy that claims the central animating element of life is power—as opposed to say, love or the Werner Herzog little-people movie—will seek power at all costs. For Nietzsche, Joy is the feeling of one's power increasing. Haven't you ever heard about the execution of the Romanovs?"

He tells me we can discuss "the Romans" another time, that he had to go, then disappears, as if he was never there to begin with.

✳

I drive along Mulholland at night to visit my dearly departed—my brother and all my dead heroes. I wear my teenage clothing, my '90s monochrome, my Ray-Bans, my slacker ennui, Nirvana's nirvana, smelling like teen spirits. Against the landscape, I count the graves in my mind, one for men, and one for a version of myself, and one for a version of my mother's self. I catch sight of myself in the mirror, that spectral mask cloaking a skeleton, lacking unity, the mirror cracking bones into sand as I disappear into Laurel Canyon, a black-clothed driver taking me on my long night's journey, no earthly star but now fully celestial.

✳

William texts from the afterlife:

these days are slated to be really stressful. astrologically, the worst time-period in years. as above—so below. any event you will into existence, or any election you craft will be imbued with very harsh energy. text me when you're dead

MADELINE

there are days where i kind of time-travel just to maintain my sanity. like today at work i overheard a patron announce that she self-identified as a "lichen," and i instantaneously hallucinated: i was suddenly at a bar in marseille and had the impression that one of my cheeks was hollowing to age and gravity. i spoke this hallucination to the bartender and was forced to leave. then i had the impression that i was on a leash being led like a dog by a double of myself with a little french mustache. at one point my double turned to me and said, "who are we?"

i admire the passion of the bloody poets, those artists who turn to suicide and insanity—"we have affronted everything we love!" but let's be real. suicide, while complex and intricate and decadent, is also indecently stupid. ultimately the poets are just like every other aquarian in this culture, whether it's oprah or ellen degeneres or jewel: satanic nymphomaniacs with borderline personality disorder.

i'm a gemini.

this evening i tried to engage with the film that guy was watching, *the astrologer*, some cult film about the second coming of jesus and astrology starring a playboy bunny. whenever i commented on the film, guy just sat there, as he does these days. ever since our dad left and became gay and proud, guy's been chemically altered in a haze of cannabis and speed, unkemptness, and vacillating levels of testosterone. not too long ago he came out as an astrologer to little fanfare.

the other day he emailed me this. even though we were both home in the same house in adjacent rooms:

Dude!

Soon, an impressive albeit frightening astrological occurrence will take shape! In anticipation, me and some art buddies are having a show to celebrate the rare and epochal configuration emerging from the hard transit of four planets: a Cardinal Grand Cross! In the face of such celestial havoc, a calamity not experienced since the winter of 863 A.D., we're gonna take refuge in a former teddy-bear factory on the outskirts of LA to show new work!

"Cardinal Cross" will be less a show than a salutation to this exceedingly rare thing. Works will range from a menagerie of suspiciously familiar recast found objects (driftwood, panties) and dead-end contraptions, to a light and sound installation as post-industrial cosmic incubator, and a bleached-out monolith festooned with the head of a Roman deity, to the refashioned remnants of funerary paraphernalia.

Can you take a look at my new bio?

"Working with various materials, my recent studio work has risen out of an ongoing exploration of the syntax of astrological space through pilgrimages made to the unfriendly corners of the San Fernando Valley."

i forgot to mention that my brother has also gotten into making miniatures. in lieu of any formal education (not that i should talk), he raids *michaels* and *joann fabrics* like an old lady from the red-hat brigade just to chip away at this weird grotto my mom had built in the backyard as a kind of children's manor. i feel alone.

   i don't know. the more i participate in the "adult" world, the more i realize what base, idiotic, self-serving monsters people can be. and that includes me. i think that's why i like satire so much. and nietzsche.

VICTORIA

Wildfires consume much of the Valley on the day of my brother's memorial.

Wandering through my mother's house, Skyla's Whispering Palms, I'm unsurprised to learn that my mother has already given away, with wild recklessness and unmatched abandon, the dead man's, my brother's, clothing. "Empty sleeves, empty shirts!" She has clothed many men in her time and had even tried with me. But I preferred the same day-in, day-out mourner's attire, monochromatic and streaked with scented-candle tallow, faded by the desert sun, without which I would barely recognize myself in the mirror.

The ears, my mother says, are great land masses no one has ever completely known or understood, echoes of echoes, reverberations and tremblings: hollow, sepulchral voices crying in their marble tombs. She's always been easily startled by sounds: ghosted footsteps in empty rooms or the whirring of a bluebird's wing against a dusty window which, long before my father left and my brother too, was draped by veils of black chiffon in memory of some earlier death she had forgotten.

*

In the entryway, there's still a framed drawing of the family I made when I was 12. The balding father, the beardless son, the delirious mother, and a terrier, Sara, named after the poet in Stevie Nicks's heart. Our Sara was our pathetic fallacy, given human characteristics she couldn't bear to hold. Will found her dying poetically in a

jacuzzi after being bitten by a rattlesnake. The drowning
was rendered in detail in the background of the drawing,
like Munch's scream without the figure—just the ambi-
ance of the scream and the background. The family leans
against the fence, fencing selves, a bridge to nowhere
against an engraved sky, grave torsos and non-sentience,
backdropped by the Valley fjords, the LA river tributar-
ies, dried out and concreted, a bridge to an accident, our
collective accidental, amidst a silent din, something unac-
countable. Somehow, I left myself out of the drawing. It
was my mother's favorite piece of art, "V's Scream" she
called it. I called it "Family."

✼

My poor mother now uses walls and trees for support,
some of which are invisible and therefore not especially
sturdy. Many times I watch her fall and get up, utterly
surprised by gravity, logic, the senses, the metaphysics
of the world. She's regressed back into childhood, where
she was a shy girl in the Valley, her best and only friend
also imaginary, Loopy Loo. And now, with nothing but
ghosts of the imaginary and the real, she's become afraid
of migrating birds, of celebrities, of ordinary people, of
those in the mirror most of all.

✼

Crystal is in full mania today, her voice becoming throat-
ier with each passing second, as though she's speaking
through a trumpet. "I just want to disappear into some
great role! Not just a janitor, or a lawyer, or a girlfriend."
Her dilated eyes stare at me. "I wanna play a real person!"

The last time we saw each other was at a holiday gathering four years ago where she brought two different men to Christmas dinner, one for dinner and one for dessert. The first man, Mayo, was indistinguishable from the second man, Melon. Even Crystal got them mixed up, not with each other, but with the other man she was seeing: Mash, her now-husband. Crystal was suffering at the time from what she characterized as a *chronic condition* which upon description sounded pretty much identical to being alive. Crystal had a mesmerizing handle on hyperbole and hyperdrama, and she could speak about the dullest topics with the gravitas of a statesman, "The bakery where I work as the Chief Entropy Officer of Guest Relationships, Begonia's Bakery, makes fennel buns." Even though she's now past 30, her face bears no marks of time, no blotches, no signs of maturity.

The distance between us—coupled with her apparent inability to even acknowledge our brother's death, even at his own memorial—makes me feel awful. I excuse myself: "Sorry. I have to go make a noose to hang myself with." Crystal guffaws and performatively yells, "You're my favorite sister!"

I am her only sister.

❋

In the carnivalesque backyard, a madwoman's wonderland, I notice how my mother is barely recognized by even the desert wildflower that had been perched in her hair, which has fallen off a waxed headband into our childhood Fairy Grotto. She had it constructed by a well-known local doll specialist.

I look into my reflection in the pool, unwigged and sexless, dead behind my green eyes, denatured, then go up to the cold buffet. There is cold bean dip, cold noodles, cold leaves, cold broth, cold cream sauces covering cold vegetables, a bowl of cold soil that contains some of my brother's ashes out of which have sprouted a single sprig of rosemary, my brother's favorite herb. But Will would have hated this memorial. He would always develop stomach aches at our gatherings, excuse himself to his room, as he couldn't digest his surroundings. His twin, I was always rather ambivalent about food, especially cold food, preferring to live off warm water.

Lacking any appetite, I place a benzodiazepine under my tongue, hoping to evaporate on the spot.

MADELINE

i'm feeling just feeling really, really sad today. and my mom's not doing any better. a few days ago she bought a few decorative plant animals (not sure how else to describe them) on sale at cvs when we went together to each get our medications. she got a small dog and what looks to be a mountain lion. she stuck them outside in her garden "to protect our jungle," she told me, and kissed my forehead like the lioness of a pride. i forgot to mention she also stuck a small bottle of sudafed she didn't pay for in her purse, but, considering not too long ago i was in a loony bin, i'm not really here to judge.

since the mother-daughter cvs outing i've spent days locked in my room and questioning everything and not speaking very much and definitely not fucking. so i guess that's whatever we call that? depression? i don't know. luckily it has been the sort of depression that has allowed me to keep working. i say luckily because although i have been feeling pretty hopeless about pretty much everything in my life, at least i'm not feeling like i'm not getting anything done on top of that. i've ended up making a little series of paintings. they are just basic paintings of little scenes from my daily life paired with quotes from beckett's *endgame*. so like a rendering of me standing naked with a paper bag over my head and a pile of trousers folded up beside me and underneath the words "but my dead sir, look at the world... and then look at my trousers." it was supposed to say "dear" but i accidentally wrote "dead."

meanwhile, my brother is banging the entire valley basin. whenever i'm depressed, he compensates by going full-on slut. he sent me an email yesterday with the subject line: "erotic lifestyle." there are seven images attached of his various hookups, culled from dating sites.

Dude!

Not sure if a "type" has emerged from my extracurricular activities so far the past month. (See attached!)

After failed attempts to start carving out more of a "life," I find myself falling back on gross licentiousness when I give up. I never get turned down, so if I can find out what it is that I do "right," perhaps then I can use "that" to actually make a life.

Anyway, here's the lineup.
1. currently wrapping herself around my finger.
2. metal head from Brazil. has a tattoo of Metallica's four horsemen on her back. best kisser, too. (you would not believe how sexy a Brazilian accent in person is)
3. fun stoner who moaned a lot.
4. white-collared freak. was totally fun.
5. super hot and had a cat named Gremlin.
6. love. like, I will be waiting for a text from this person for the rest of my life and beyond.
7. pure sociopathological evil.

Look, I started working out and have for the moment stopped drinking, so what else am I supposed to do

with my time? It's like being in prison when you say
"well, fuck it, i'm just gonna get cut cuz i'm in a shitty
place and can just drown everything out through
body improvement." Or something dumb like that.

Absorb the vibes, dude!

"jesus we're both what modern medicine might call crazy,"
i wrote back.

but at least he's back to talking to me, even if it's
only virtually.

VICTORIA

If people think of lesbians, they think of something dis-agreeable, and they're not wrong. This is why culture makes us invisible. But I actually like being invisible. I like hiding in the aisles of stores whenever I spot some-one I know before they can look right through me. I grab my painkillers and my peanut butter cups and dodge their gaze.

*

All my failures are up for grabs. My disappointments, all the fallen stars and bottles of Everclear I've wept into, how last night I smashed a bottle over my vintage copy of *A Visit to 13 Asylums for the Insane in Europe*, a book my brother and I revered because it was about a journey-man's visit to some women's asylum in Venice and included the color-coding of pathologies, where residents were forced to wear the colors of their pathologies or "species of insanity," so that mine, for example — "melancholy" — was Green, while my brother's color was the moody Deep Blue of "delusional disorder," and we reverse-diagnosed our father with "idiotismo" as his favorite color was Orange. We loved this interplay between fate and archi-tecture, between insanity and context, and would as children pretend that the Fairy Grotto was the Venetian Asylum, where the insane of any color would intermin-gle. It was our utopia.

*

Before we went crazy, Will and I would converse for hours, in the safe space of a friendship spanning our entire lives, many years, a few boyfriends, a few girlfriends, and the loss of our father to Europe and our mother's faculties to the ravages of time, age, carcinogenic plastic packages of mustard, flanked by family hairlessness and blurring gray daisies, fading pixels uploaded to the clouds.

MADELINE

i'm not exactly doing a hat dance these days, though a few really good things happened to me today. i got a raise at whole foods and my health insurance arrived in the mail, but nevertheless i am feeling strangely ill at ease tonight. i'm not sure why. something ominous. like knowing death exists but only in the abstract. even though i cannot express how strongly i believe that ignorance is bliss, but with equal conviction i also believe that half-knowing is insanity.

anyway i bought vegan cookies to try in celebration of my higher paycheck: "back to nature" brand california lemon cookies, which are unnaturally lemony and delicious. i was making them into a pyramid display at the store and had to put up this sign my manager made that said "enjoy yourself." he's trying to get into advertising. anyway, as i was propping up the sign with a box of cookies, an attractive older brunette woman, maybe mid-20s, maybe late-20s, pointed to the sign and said "does that refer to the masturbatory act?" something about the way she said it, i don't know. i keep eating the cookies and can't stop thinking about her.

i'd say i've reached a new low, but considering i spent the prior night in groucho marx glasses watching the marx brothers, i guess it's just par for the course (i have no idea what that cliché actually means, golf-wise or whatever).

VICTORIA

I can't believe I've been forced to come back to suburbia. I'm like my neighbor, a former child star, who's allowing her own supple body to age like a fine wine, like an old Italian movie star eating softened chocolate with a baby spoon. Or maybe the chocolate is funneled into an old squeeze bottle and hosed directly into her mouth, something I heard someone talk about doing in a Grow Your Own Drugs class I once took out of curiosity at the YMCA. In Last Chance. Iowa.

✳

My favorite student Aron emails me a note of condolence about my brother, saying he and all the students miss me, and that they can't wait for me to come back in the fall to teach my seminar on "the closeted homosexuals." Aron has attached an image of himself to the email holding a chicken at a Mennonite farm, smiling, like a proud father. He ends the note with a poem fragment:

you always talked to yourself
sitting under a fig tree with leaves
words of your mother tongue
in the tongue of your previous self
of your alternate self

to ingest them
make them your own
like a chicken nibbling the ear of a book

I go to my mother's garage to clean out Will's stuff. Skyla stays inside watching a television show about things people put inside their rear ends: Mrs. Butterworth bottles, spicy Italian sausage, pepper mills, stilettos. "You should see these clowns under a microscope!" she calls to me as I head to the garage, though I'm pretty sure she means X-ray.

I look at Will's participation trophies, books about Dennis Hopper and the bombing of Hiroshima, CDs of his failed music projects, old canisters of black-and-white film, and a pair of checkered Vans with a hole where his big toe chafed through. I toss all of this into a trash bag slated for Goodwill, knowing full well it will sit in the trunk of my car forever.

Behind my mother's painting of Bobby Fisher being attacked by his chess pieces that's propped against the wall, I see a box labeled "V's Crap." I open it up and discover: it is indeed crap. But amongst the papers, photographs, and locks of Sara the dog's hair, is a Venetian marbleized box that triggers me.

Right before he left for Italy for good, our father gave my brother and me each one of these Venetian marbleized boxes. Attached to the boxes were identical notes: "I'll forever be waiting for your well wishes, your outpourings of gifts, and assistance in matters of my livelihood!" The boxes were empty. "Until then, save every photograph I send to you!"

Will tossed his box in the trash and never thought about it again. I saved my box, hiding it in my mother's garage where it's sat for years, accruing all the photographs our father sent us until he stopped, staged images of himself lounging in front of various wonders of the world—the opera house in Sydney, the pyramids of Egypt, a giant phallus of volcanic rock in Cappadocia. I would stare at every photo after it arrived, trying to create some kind of emotional circuitry between the image of him and myself. Without fail, I only ever ended up feeling like a solitary depressive in an Edward Hopper diner.

✳

I stare at a picture of myself at nineteen that my mom gave me that was on Will's desk: I'm wearing black-on-black-on-black at the Santa Monica pier, drinking gin from a straw out of a to-go cup. When I was younger, I was described as Salma Hayek meets Minnie Driver meets some gay woman who died of rectal cancer on an episode of a show whose name no one could ever recall.

That was right around the time I met Dora, during an especially slow and brown summer, when snakes were lounging everywhere, the pathetic LA River bubbling up and thickening. My father had fled us to explore himself, money was scarce, and I was working at a health food store on Riverside that used to be called Mrs. Gooch's Natural Foods Market but that Whole Foods had recently bought and it smelled like warmed cabbage and powdered vitamins.

All my human dreck was pretty inconsequential to the drought-intolerant sunflowers we carried in the store. But Dora noticed. I was fragile and anemic at the time but Dora seemed to want the responsibility. She was older and more comfortable with her sexuality. She was a bit of a hater and seemed to like my discontent, and maybe she thought it would be interesting to date someone with an overactive, explorative brain. The first time we met she made an off-hand comment when I tried to get her to taste a sample of a new vegan lentil loaf we were selling, "Bullshit is a creative act," she smirked. I felt nervous and excited when she said it. I turned the color of the nearby organic eggplant and clammed up. I never felt this with men. I never felt much of anything with men, I realized, and I somehow thought that meant I was straight.

✳

Now, at 42, I feel like a scallion left in the back of the fridge. My face has become a death mask falling off its own skull, gesturing toward the underworld. I've never had the kind of eyelashes that feather across lids, floral parasols to protect against harsh elements, but only recently did I notice I have been shedding. My limbs are no longer waif-like, but my ponytail is skinnier than ever. I place massage balls against my back when I'm driving.

✳

In some of my darkest hours, I remember with fondness my first kiss with Dora, and especially her throbbing, persistent tongue. It was medically huge.

I keep a toiletry bag containing things Dora left behind: a tiny comb, her signature cologne. She used to love me to comb her hair, what was left of it after her Wellbutrin overdose. I often splash the cologne over my face vigorously. Sometimes even using it as a mouthwash. Dr. Nicky found all of this "curious."

✳

I half-sleep and dream I'm on a plane in my mother's backyard. "They" won't let me off. The poke of a finger emerges from the soft, blurred background on the interior. My father, the pilot, raises an eyebrow, tosses back the set of pearls around his neck, and turns his elbow. Somehow I know this means I can never return home. I wake up and write a mantra on the mirror: "Exhaustion helps you think."

MADELINE

when i tell people my sister jewel is an aspiring actress they think of a young chlöe sevigny. they do not think of someone with a recurring role on television as "freakishly tall girl at prom." but that's who jewel is.

currently jewel is outside on a small stage she's made for herself, dressed as the musical character annie. she sings the line—"i don't need sunshine now to turn my skies to blue!"—then dramatically jumps off the stage straight onto the ground. she stays there for a few seconds, then shakes it off, gets up, and repeats the actions. she's clearly locked into some kind of private death ritual.

jewel is kind of a miracle, and i have moments of intense envy at her level of confidence. she has a heightened self-seriousness that coming from any other person would read as self-parody. for example she told me today after trying out for the role of "pregnant alien girl at a prom": "what we do as artists is so fucking difficult! you are constantly putting yourself out there! laying bare your soul!!"

"artists"? "soul"? the soul of what? jewel used to bug me a lot. but i've recently taken a different approach to our hangouts: open to the experience, curious, heavily drugged. so today when she told me about her struggles as an artist, i was all "yes sister preach tell me more." being on her level is its own kind of high. escaping reality through storytelling is rather fun it turns out.

or maybe i was just in a good mood because that 20-something brunette came into whole foods again today. she made an amusing comment about this brownish lentil-and-rice sloppy joes special we were selling: "this gravedigger special looks compost-inspired. i'll take one for here and one to go!" she smiled, but i couldn't tell what on earth was making her happy. her energy was intriguing, like she'd just been reincarnated or is a visual artist. also her lips were full and beautiful and her mouth always seems to be a bit ajar. her name is dora, "as in freud," she told me. if i'm being totally honest, i fainted a little when she said it.

VICTORIA

Yesterday a concerned neighbor called to tell me my mother was spotted in a lawn chair on her porch yelling at two children in matching jumpsuits who weren't there.

✳

I go to my mother's and find her napping in a lounge chair in a purple childlike dress, her hands resting in her lap on a piece of parmesan in a plastic baggie and a pink Sharpie. On the table beside her is a photo of me as a child, dressed as Sherlock Holmes and wearing a monocle, examining a variety of geodes with the magnifying glass over my eye. There is a white Post-it Note attached to it with pink handwriting: "Lesbian-in-training."

✳

Crystal appears outside with her husband Mash as I'm throwing coins in the Fairy Grotto.

"Sorry, Vic," Mash says to me. Crystal had recently eloped with Mash. With his mulish looks, a drooping mouth the color of bubblegum, and barely sentient bovine eyes, he is the perfect mate for my sister.

It's unclear if he's sorry about my brother's death, sorry for being there, sorry for existing, or just hungry. Mash taps Crystal to stop her twitching and hands me the contents of his pockets—magic mushrooms—then goes back inside. Crystal hooks me into her latest traumatic plot involving a run-in on the street with a dirty orphan as though it is a scene from *Les Misérables*. Crystal, the same girl who not too long ago I remember lying on the floor kicking her legs when she wanted candy, trying to rid herself of the almost deadly boredom exhibited in many people under the age of 40. I respect her for this innate ability to find drama in the everyday.

Poor thing is six foot three, but that's never stopped her from trying to land the part. "I've alwaaaaays loveeeed looooove!" she croons, as she sing-songs her way through the tale of an orphan who came into Begonia's Bakery asking for day-old croissants. Crystal emerged from behind the counter and interviewed her on the spot on what the word "love" meant to an orphan. "Sheee didn't have a cluueeee!" Crystal crooned like a hotel-lobby chanteuse and made a glissando gesture across her invisible piano, "Nooo pastriiies for heeeerrr." I wondered how Crystal knew this person was an orphan and not just poor and Crystal asked me to define the difference: "Defiiiineee pleaaaasse."

All I can think is, "This is why I will never have children." I think of Will, who also didn't want children, and how he would have been amused by Crystal's crooning.

Crystal abruptly ends her musical-theater warpath. She comments on my thinning hair, like our brother's and our mother's, too, our familial baldness, our giant combover. She says she wishes her hair would one day, too, thin so that she could feel closer to us, but in the meantime, she's happy to feel unaffiliated with our hairlessness and that she has a recommendation for a glossy tonic, not to mention skin-brightening cream, a mascara harvested from silkworms, neck acid, and something called Face Erasure. It is remarkable how Californians so easily allow themselves to be swallowed up by purity and Fascism.

My mother asks the cock-eyed Fairy doll in the Grotto who's supposed to be my fairy doppelgänger, "Why are children so cruel to their mothers?"

※

My mom once told me the bravest thing she had ever done in her life was to audition for her junior high's Hootenanny. She had been taking guitar and singing lessons, and she had a fantasy that she was going to be Joni Mitchell. This was based on no known reality at all in her life. I suppose this is where Crystal got her delusions. She was painfully shy, and her teachers at one point thought she was mute. This was all compounded by the fact that her parents were extraordinarily strict, so she wasn't allowed to shave her legs, pluck her eyebrows, eat ice cream with her friends after school, or wear a skirt that cut above her hairy knees. She wore ice-blue glasses and was called Four Eyes. But somehow, my mother, despite all this, thought she could be a star.

She waited in the wings with her guitar next to a popular jock named Darrell before going on stage in front of the entire school, the largest public school in the Valley. Darrell had just performed an energetic version of the Doors' "Light My Fire" so it was a tough act to follow. My mother, in her little dress my grandmother had sewn for her with a prominent collar and a seam that fell to the earth, got up on her little stool. Her knees knocked together. She swallowed hard and steadied herself. And proceeded to perform a very uninspired rendition of Peter, Paul, and Mary's iconic "Leaving on a Jet Plane." The response from the crowd was minimal. She never performed again.

Now looking at the Fairy Grotto, looking at my mother and feeling the grip of life, I realize the bravest thing someone can do isn't an awkward rendition of a '60s classic. It's getting old, dealing with loss and death, burying a child, and somehow, pulling through. I can feel the presence of that little awkward girl inside her now, wanting to get off the stage, but, somehow, singing off-key until the very end.

I go to my mom and try to take her hand in mine. To bring that young girl toward me. She waves my hand away.

MADELINE

"so my friend stevie and one of her annoying friends from high school were singing 'silver springs' when i arrived at the karaoke bar," my mom tells me. "and once they finished, i grabbed this hilarious jewish dude at the next table and we sang michael bolton's 'how am i supposed to live without you' but sang it amazingly well. it was hilarious! it was seriously one of my greatest achievements."

i had no idea my mom liked karaoke. or had a friend named stevie. or was she referring to stevie nicks? was stevie nicks at the bar singing her own songs? was my mom ever at the bar at all?

"actually," my mom said, "i take it back. to lose your partner and your mother, be inundated with fake celebrities and burning bushes, to find yourself in a new world changing at an unprecedented pace—i believe my greatest achievement is staying alive."

right then jewel came in eating a tureen of chocolate ice cream and asked if we liked her new cutoff pink shirt that said "sluts unite" and winked at me. i'll never recover. from any of it.

You can never return to your childhood. It's simply never there. In its place a void, nothingness. Not the absence of something, just nothing-nothingness, utter blankness, non-meaning, non-place: the San Fernando Valley, a vast expanse whose sole mission is to contribute to the waning role of architecture and refined taste in modern life. Its Contempo Casual aesthetics and loose morals are said to be derived from that famous European painting school called Abortion. As you sit in your air-conditioned vehicle moving less than the speed of life, you realize all of your own idiocy seems to be distilled into its very essence. You're not there, either.

VICTORIA

I walk up and down the block of Ventura Boulevard that used to house my optometrist, a spot called I&Joy Bagels, a surplus store where mom bought us superhero Underoos, and the diner where we had pancake breakfasts while my brother used a toy gun to shoot everyone in the restaurant. That place no longer exists.

In its space is a glittery pink sign that reads: *ASTROLOGER (Gemini)*.

✳

When I first met Dora, I was at a kind of low point in my life where I believed astrology was real, and so I believed in Dora and in us: a Gemini like myself, twinning all over the place. Over time, I realized she abstained from many things, including common sense. She didn't eat meat, not cow because they were spotted and she liked piebald animals, not fowl because she had a feather fetish, not fish because she once had a guppy named Moby Dick with the face of Jesus on its scales, but somehow she would eat eggs compulsively, the unborn, with great enthusiasm. I adored her.

One day, Dora began to have strange premonitions. She dreamt that she went to a mechanic because a stray cat she had found was "broken" and asked if he provided service for cats, and the man, a sexy heterosexual said no that wasn't his thing but that Dora could try buying tuna fish in oil, and, by the time she got home, to our home in the dream, which she described as having the energy of a podiatrist's office, the cat was dead in our bedroom.

From then on, so was our sex life.

She began to make little jabs at me, like "Dating you is a cross between Enid from *Ghost World* and Sarah Silverman," and "It's not as fun as it sounds." Ideally, I would have preferred to be more like a cross between Peter Sellers and Vladimir Nabokov. Then she admitted to cheating on me.

I remember one shameful moment toward the end when I wrote her a letter and sent it through the mail because I thought it would be romantic. "I'm still in love with you, and I will always be in love with you, but I'll take what you are willing to give me and be more than happy with it." Will helped me write it. He was just as hopeless a romantic as I was.

"Love can take away all aspects of death," I told him, "but I think I might be hopeless."

"Don't worry, V. Everything happens twice," I remember her saying to me, "we tell the same two stories our entire lives."

✱

I wander out to the derelict outdoor mall on Laurel Canyon near Victory. I pass a broken gym, the busted storefront of a teddy-bear store, the crumbling Italianate ruins of the Spaghetti Sauce Factory. In the empty parking lot, a driver doing wheelies in a limo yells out, "Mad, bad, and dangerous to know!" He could have been talking about the British Romantic, Lord Byron. But he was looking at me when he said it.

MADELINE

i'm back… with a mouthful of tomato sauce. i realized just the other day that in my head i often first pronounce it with a british accent, toe-mah-toe, then translate it into american english. i don't think i realized i did this at all until yesterday when i pronounced it the brit way and got a very quizzical look from dora at the health food store. of course, i still have no idea if she's single or what end of the twenties spectrum she falls into, but she seems a bit interested, and fuck, has things to say about beckett and death. today she said to me "you can't expect the world to share the burden of the heavy stuff—you'll scare them all away." it was like listening to myself but a version of myself or a version of myself i found hot. and maybe that's not even what she said, because like every other person in this television town i've mastered the art of projection. and as sad as that might sound, it is true, and she was right. people don't want to hear about sad stuff, they have better things to do. and i don't expect i'd feel any better without any friends. so i told dora i'm only just learning to give more of the positive and less of the negative. i'm getting by. i'm going one minute at a time, one drug at a time. i'll go on. i have to go on… i think she thinks i'm too crazy to want to bang me. but in any case i think all this anglophilia goes back to my lady english teacher in high school who i had a crush on, who taught me about the overlap between the digestive system, the intellect, raging teenage sexuality, and how everything sounded better in the queen's english than in american.

i guess i'm now not so sure it's men i'm even innately attracted to. i've always had much more interesting, emotional, and intense relationships with women. but maybe that has more to do with women than with sexuality? who knows.

i'm not sure how i should write this next part because it doesn't address the content in the previous, so i'm just starting a new paragraph. but i guess the fact that i've taken to writing a rambling missive is a good sign. it has really been bothering me that i haven't felt the slightest urge to write. all i've done this week is just massive amounts of lying around and smoking hash and eating grapes and buying antique knick-knacks. it has been especially frustrating because it's not exactly like i don't have anything to work on. i have a play, the one about the bored seraphim, that needs major hammering out but still has a chance of being halfway decent. but that's barely work i guess.

so i am making pasta... like, just plain old straight pasta with tomato sauce from the jar and nothing else. now that out i'm out of the asylum, i can do whatever i please without the "protein police" getting all up on my snatch.

VICTORIA

Eating rice noodles with ketchup (empty calories) and watching reruns of *The L Word* (more empty calories) reminds me that if there is one thing I have resented every day it is my sexuality. Lesbianism confers no evolutionary advantage: the over-processing, raging hormones, intellectual poverty, haircuts that mimic toupees, the inhuman dancing at softball gatherings, voices like the bleating of a sad zoo pony in a purple skirt, mothers of unhappy endings.

*

I discovered my sexuality when I mentally placed myself in front of a girl and imagined kissing her. The result was an array of physical and psychological symptoms, overwhelming desire mixed with just the right amount of shame to make it hot. I concluded I was a relationship person because that's where my fantasies always ended: Years before I lost my virginity to a woman, I spooned pillows and brushed their shaggy hair-like trim, chatting with my imaginary others about gardening, books, and cooking. I've always wanted to know women, to explore their proclivities and wounds. I've been entranced by all their weird stuff, their crying when fucking, their vainglorious self-deprecation. I once had this domestic side I wanted to cultivate, carve out some special terrain with another woman. Clearly, I had no regard for the truth. Later, I realized I wasn't a relationship person, but someone with an overly active imagination.

*

Now when I witness rampant displays of lesbianism, I think not of progress but of a society on the verge of imminent collapse. Of the atrocities of Nero, Caligula, Annie Leibovitz. Of Cara Delevingne's *Architectural Digest* interview Dora made me watch, in which she says, and I paraphrase: "This is my sex room. On the ceiling you'll notice a photo of my mother breastfeeding me, and here is where I climb back into the womb."

Among many other dreamy clichés, Dora was an artist, like my mother was once. She showed me her paintings of women wrapped tightly around one another, or maybe wrestling. They had oversized toes and painted nails and their mouths were in the shape of dollar signs which I think had something to do with feminism. The paint on their skin was peeling off. Dora told me the paintings were of her and her ex, a younger lover. I told her I wanted to be like her ex, but before the ex became an ex. "My gallery says my paintings are getting too violent and homophobic but also too lesbian." I told her I got it, which I didn't, and asked her how long she had been at the whole self-destructive thing and she said, stoned and a little bored, "Forever. I take my time with it. Anything worth doing is worth doing slowly." I wasn't sure if she was talking about suicide or sex, but in my head, they were the same. I wanted her to steal me from myself.

✳

I look at these toxic coupled lesbians roaming the streets and thank God for exploring celibacy over the past few years. In the seventeenth century, the only option for an intellectual was to become a nun—or kill yourself.

Conversely, in the early twenty-first century, celibacy is the heretical move and I am all for it, pressing mute on eros and wrapping it in a monastic death shroud.

But let's be honest, and by "let's" I mean let me: deep down I'm afraid to give up abstinence for fear I'll fall right back into some pretty debased patterns that haunted my 20s, and which trickled into my thirties. This is why I'm okay with things not working out with that lesbian poet who came to visit who only ate meatballs, or with the young check-out girl at the Hy-Vee in Iowa City who I had a minor crush on for a week because she quoted Iggy Pop lyrics to me. Turns out, she was an MFA poetry student of mine and I didn't recognize her in her "costume." In any case, I'm not sure I want to go back to sex ever. Once I gave up on sex, I became obsessed with writing poetry and British-like comedies around the same time. A creative spurt that, come to think of it, may have been occasioned by playing chemist with my medicine again rather than not fucking.

My new order of preference for company is: Heterosexual Woman at the top and Lesbian Woman at the bottom, with uncategorizable mish-mash and houseplants in between.

❋

Sometimes I throw up my "fuck it!" hands. Sometimes failure isn't some gay radical act.

The real world goes like this: the jagged edges of the Valley's mountains scrape the sky like broken glass, cleaving the LA basin in two. You swerve along Mulholland Drive, dodging the occasional paparazzo and coyote. Where the range meets the Pacific, the most terrifying of oceans, Highway 1 slithers. Sometimes you find seashells in the mountain canyons though there hasn't been an ocean there for thousands of years. Sometimes when you walk along the trails in your skin-tight misery garb you think you see a celebrity with an eating disorder or an eating disorder masquerading as a celebrity. In the middle of your path, a rogue diamondback rattlesnake molts like a child taking off a knee-high sock—you run in the opposite direction, nibbling anxiously on your protein brick, nibbling for your life.

MADELINE

i'm like jean genet who didn't even go to a screening of the adaptation of his own book *querelle* because "you can't smoke at the movies."

what i mean is, i'm becoming a french homosexual. my crush dora asked me to get frozen yogurt and i was inspired to get healthy beforehand and have now been 48 hours without a cigarette and i'm dying. i noticed there is this weird thing that happens when your body is craving nicotine: you become slightly retarded. i've been going around all day basically functioning on the same level that i do when i'm drunk… and i'm not even drunk. the whole thing becomes an intricate process of distracting yourself. maybe this is how jewel feels all the time.

i think i need to immerse myself in some art or writing project, but i don't know what. i'm just too ill-equipped to cope with life without cigarettes or caffeine or marijuana or speed. i can't get through a day without drugs.

yesterday i went to my grandmother's wake. helen looked desiccated and fragile in her forever-nightgown. not fragile on the "glass" end of the spectrum, but straw-like, a colored husk from an outdoor thanksgiving decor blowout at michaels. basically a mummification that's been moistened with a bunch of liquid foundation, a dried floral arrangement that's sat untouched for decades on a table, only to be covered in cobwebs. and the hands just looked horrible, similar to dried latex. helen was an avid painter so there were framed pieces of hers surrounding the casket and floral arrangements: a portrait of her dog, a portrait of her grandchildren, a portrait of my mother being attacked by birds of prey. it was actually really lovely and life-affirming.

my mother gave a beautiful, though slightly incoherent speech about the "ashen prune-child sleeping in her crate" (grandmom). she lit a candle over helen and said: "light is illuminating and dazzling, it draws the eye into a painting, creates shadows and contours. it warms and chills." then we ate my grandmother's favorite cheese-filled pastries. i saw my mom leave her body.

afterward, my mom gave me a bag of items my grandmother wanted me to have, whispering in my ear: "please don't re-sell them."

my grandmother left me loads of her costume jewelry and a real chinchilla fur coat. at first i was horrified by the fur but tonight i tried it on and honestly i just feel so glamorous and cool, like marianne faithful or jerry hall or any other woman who has ever dated mick jagger. then i put on this giant lion medallion necklace i kind of love and began to pair it with jeans and other boring items, but got overwhelmed and decided i needed inspiration. so now i'm listening to purple haze, wishing my grandma were here with me, drinking her gin and tonic, and talking to me about the pope.

VICTORIA

It's 4 am, I am drinking seed oil, touching receipts from the pharmacy for pills and power bars, and slathering myself in SPF 100 sunscreen. I'm wondering: Am I a ghost or a badass or badass's ghost?

✳

Right before Dora and I broke up, she tried to get me into yoga. I think it was an attempt to help vivify our sex life, which somehow had gone missing, a mystery novel called *Lesbian Bed Death*.

I built us a new bed that faced a new window, re-world-ing our bedroom. The San Gabriel mountains spun off the arm of the cosmos into the void that window framed. *What a view!* Dora exclaimed.

We began having crazed fights about everything from disliking the ways oatmeal can be prepared—cold versus baked versus stovetop versus cookies versus savory versus is this bird feed versus feed-feed versus papi-er-mâché comic goop prosthesis poking at oxygen—or whether it is ever ethical for a child to get braces. You know you're at the end of your relationship when after a fight concludes, you are devastated not because the relationship is over, but because it still exists.

A few months after the oatmeal fight, and many other fights that had nothing to do with food, my grandmother died, which didn't help to minimize my obsession with illness and death. We both started rapid cycling after that, trading off mania and depression like a hot potato.

I remember leaving a note on our kitchen table: "We can't have you in such a state where you are bashing your head against the floor until it bleeds." The note, in retrospect, was not only insane but about me.

Afterward, I couldn't sleep in the room, where once I wasn't alone. It swelled with memory. It sucked the oxygen out of me. So did the French cigarettes I had begun smoking again when I was with Dora.

✺

I send Aron an uncharacteristically sentimental email about how much I miss him, my other students, teaching, and the chickens of Iowa. Aron emails me back this quote followed by five <3's:

> *The writings on the pages are in my mind, the writings in my brain are in the air and the letters are in suspense. —Asaf Halet* Çelebi, *Books*

MADELINE

my brother is a feminist and i can often respect that. last night, though, he was saying how horrible the fashion industry is for making women feel like they need to be impossibly thin. honestly it annoyed the shit out of me.

in my opinion, this is pretty much a non-issue. that's the way that it is, and it's not going to change. what needs to change is that women need to stop feeling bad about themselves if they don't look like high fashion models. unless, i guess, if you are an aspiring fashion model, but most women aren't.

fashion designers show their clothing on super-skinny women because clothing hangs better on women shaped like clothing racks—that is a fact. you can't blame a designer for wanting his or her collections to hang properly and look the way he or she intended it to look! if women want to translate it as "this is how beautiful women should look," that's their problem. most fashion designers are gay men or straight women, who, all things considered, probably offer the least credible opinion when it comes to knowing what makes a woman sexually desirable. they want their clothes to look good, end of story. it's not personal.

if women want to evaluate their own sexual attractiveness based on the types of girls that people who aren't even attracted to women choose to use to display their clothing, then women are just being insane and looking for another reason to feel bad about themselves. as if we need another reason!

i don't know. maybe my brother is right and i'm just a dreadful feminist. but speaking of women stuffing their faces, i'm embarrassed to say i'm pretty excited to get froyo with dora.

VICTORIA

A few days or weeks or months after the memorial, Dora shows up at Skyla's, looking at me as though I'm a posse of lost souls and not one tiny, increasingly emaciated lesbian, like I represent melancholy itself, which I suppose is somewhat true.

It reminds me of when we first met over two decades ago. That first date night, after I got off from Mrs. Gooch's, we walked to a froyo place I can't remember the name of. There were so many. At the time, most of the Valley subsisted on frozen yogurt, which in retrospect is pretty odd and not exactly the mark of a great culture. Dora took me to her weird Germanic house in the hills, which I later learned her parents had gotten her because they were rich enough to use actual money as emotional currency. The whole setup was neo-modernist and a little communist.

I was pretty nervous when we got inside because I sensed I was no longer in control of anything. I remember Dora went to the kitchen, grabbed a single fresh ginkgo leaf, and presented it, like a splayed camel's toe, to me, asking me to admire all the different ways to open up the world. She then chewed it whole and said something about it counteracting the effects of smog on the body or something. I was intrigued by Dora's botanical wisdom, her ivy tendrils of knowledge. She lit a joint, inhaled slowly, and passed it between our mouths, like the ocean's vapor heat.

She must have sensed my teen angst and hormonal surge because Dora blew more marijuana into my mouth and then undressed me. She took her head in her hands and said, "Self-destruction is boring. Let's destroy each other." I could feel her hot breath. She took the lioness pendant around my neck into her mouth and gently sucked on it. She grabbed my ponytail and my nerves felt sharp. My internal monologue shut off and I stopped editing the scene in my head. I watched her lower lip without moving, wanting but not touching. My silence was part of our lust contract. I let her consume me.

Before I left, Dora gave me a sachet filled with ginkgo leaf, glow-in-the-dark discontinued nail-polish colors (lavender, seafoam, aurora borealis), diet pills, and exact replicas of St Paul's crucifixion nails (her favorite martyr, he was crucified upside-down), all somehow signifying man's sacrifice for meaning. She told me she once starved herself for a week in solidarity with some homeless cats she found roaming behind a Subway, which seemed like an excessive way to politicize her anorexia. In fact, she was starving all the time. But so was I.

Dora I guess has come today to pay her condolences about my brother. She always found my family irresistible: "I love Whispering Palms, but your people are wacko," she once famously said, as I tossed rocks back into the Pacific on my particularly moody 20th birthday. One minute it was tears, the next minute we were laughing. We did that for way too long.

"I'm finally on a mood stabilizer cocktail," Dora says, as we're standing in Skyla's backyard.

"That's great. I'm really happy for you," I say, watching as my mother puts a bouquet of dead roses from the funeral into a vase filled with water.

"Jogging, evening primrose oil, brain-spotting, weed," she says. "Oh, and Vyvanse."

I stare at a bee dying in the Fairy Grotto.

"I'm sorry I couldn't come to the funeral. I'm trying out radical honesty: I had to go to a cacao ceremony in Costa Rica that I had booked months ago. Anyways, I'm sorry I made so many mistakes when we were together. You made mistakes, too. But I made more," she says.

Time keeps dumping me overboard, pelting me with the occasional life preserver, but Dora still haunts me with her long pale face, her frisky tits, her shrewd fingers singed from darkroom chemicals. I can't be lured back.

Though she looks genuinely sad today, I know how susceptible I am to cult leaders.

"Thank you for coming to visit us. It means a lot," I say, squeezing her arm. And I leave her, just like that, and go in search of a piece of cheese leftover from the memorial buffet.

She calls after me: "I'm genuinely sorry for being a weirdo to you, Vic!"

MADELINE

i've been painfully introspective the last few days. it has been really hot, and mom for some reason hasn't had a chance to fix the air conditioner. though i doubt "chance" has anything to do with this.

in any case, to get out of my head and out of the heat, i went on my date with dora. we walked to yoghurt yoghurt, the humbert humbert of frozen yogurt parlors. "i say that not only because the brand name is in duplicate but because it's staffed by teenage girls who want to get us all in jail for staring at their pristine skin."

"aren't *you* a teenage girl?" dora said.

dora tried five different flavors, which seemed to ruffle the girls. i ordered the vegan chocolate because that was the only vegan option other than just getting a cup of sprinkles.

"are you like afraid of pesticides or germs in dairy?" dora asked, licking her spoon of dairy.

"i'm not a germaphobe. i'm just a hypochondriac. i really only get worked up about the terminal stuff," i said.

"like what? cancer?" she asked.

"no cancer's treatable. i mean mostly stuff like death," i said, plunging my spoon into the melted chocolate oil.

"but there's so much to live for! there's frozen fucking yogurt. there's lesbianism. life's pretty good," she said to me.

"i guess. but like today. after work, i spent two hours researching the average monthly residential kilowatt usage, learning how to calculate a kilowatt based on the wattage of any given appliance, going around the apartment and finding out the wattage of all of my appliances and lights, and calculating my approximate kilowatt usage per appliance per month. just because the electricity bill came and i opened it mistaking it for a letter from my father, who i haven't heard from in many months. but like, i wasn't concerned about it being inaccurate or about saving money or energy or anything like that...i was just curious," i said to her.

dora stared at me. she looked, i'm not sure how to say this but: aroused.

"and all the while i was digging into a jar of trader joe's organic unsweetened apple sauce. in my bathrobe. with olive oil in my hair," i said, which i realized sounded more seductive than i had intended.

dora pushed her yogurt aside, and i immediately felt very weird.

"anyway, sometimes i feel like it's a no-brainer why i have such a hard time convincing other people to like me," i said, licking my spoon, batting my eyelashes, playing lolita.

and then, just like that, dora dora kissed me at yoghurt yoghurt.

VICTORIA

When was the last time you kissed someone, and why?
I hear myself say out loud to the Fairy Grotto. An attractive, slim-hipped woman responds: "You have to be Will's sister."

The woman in front of me is William's girlfriend of a few years, Sasha, a wiry, pretty, ombre blonde with lively blue, freckled eyes. Her eyewear says Crap on the side of it. Her mouth has a lovely upturn. She is someone I want to tell all my secrets to immediately.

"Sorry, I used to be good at remembering everything, including how to meet new people, but I think I lost some of my instincts over the last few months."

"Yeah, I get it," she says to me. "It's amazing how much of your brain sadness takes up."

I almost faint.

Why did I never meet her before? I guess because I never went home and William had become afraid of traveling and many other things, and I had stopped caring. God, am I dumb. My mom was always boasting about Sasha to me, that she was a famous screenwriter. Apparently, she had written a film called *Ponder Ward*, a low-tech thriller set in a nursing home. But mostly she is a psychotherapist doing something called "narrative therapy" and loved my brother.

"You're still in Iowa?" she asks me. Most of the time people ask me about Ohio or Idaho, which I've never been to but have heard nice things about. I was touched that she knew what state I was living in.

"Well not right now. Or am I? I've been having trouble with space and time."

"You remind me a lot of your brother," she says. "We're at your mom's house."

"Right, right. Thought so. I was teaching in Iowa, not sure if I still am. It's, you know, very Iowan, very flyover state, but charming in its own way. There are chickens and hogs and writers and sorority girls. Sometimes you can smell meth being made in the cornfields. We have a few local lunatics who wander the streets. Sometimes one of them is me." I sound like Fuckhead from *Jesus's Son*. "Just kidding," I say, trying to lessen the idiocy.

Sasha smiles. "You're making me miss Will."

Women have an innate ability to rescue me from the hell of loneliness, daring me out of my revolting death hole. I want to talk to her about the miseries of the Contemporary Situation, the boredom I hear permeating the lives of young people, the meaningless and pathetic rituals that secularism has wrought, so that as a mourner in a modern urban landscape one has a choice between the godlessness of a peyote ceremony in the desert among the robots or sneaking into a house of worship at night dressed as an assassin to smash the head of a statue of Saint Francis not realizing that he represents not the patriarchy but the love of all God's creatures, never allowing yourself to meditate and light small candles to the subtle resonances that exist in between fear of death and paying someone your life's savings to be castrated.

But I get nervous and instead, point out a pair of ladies' underwear in the Grotto. "Did you see these panties?"

Sasha explains that my mother had allowed a "homeless woman," who in a fit of psychosis was a purported descendent of Lot's wife, to sleep in the Fairy Grotto, the same place where my brother and I played as children, which now served as a metaphor of decay. "Your mom's going through something. I guess she has been for a while."

Now that I was back, I would find some fairy worker to take care of the Fairy Grotto, to make sure it was refurbished, the fairies polished, the tiny furniture regrommeted. I sense that I am now in charge, the man of the house, a lesbian. Looking at the dilapidated miniature wine cellar and pill cozy that we had to help the fairies through hard fairy times, I can see that childhood is over, that I can never go back to the Grotto, the ghost residence of fairies.

MADELINE

today, out of nowhere, i bought rosary beads. the same style ones my mom has had since she was a teenager and wore to a school talent show, back when she wanted to be a backup singer for peter, paul, and mary. sometimes i still catch her singing when she's painting in the garage. she's working on this really interesting series that fuses our family history and mythology. practically this means she's painting a portrait of me being saved by jesus just liked he saved peter from drowning. i don't think i'm in dire straits (maybe it's not supposed to be me?) but i do appreciate the use of collage as divine wish fulfillment.

anyway, the point is, between the painting and my new favorite rosary, it seems we've both been having a religious awakening.

like this evening i've been locked in my room reading *revelations*. i can't get over the bit where saint john is describing all of the shit that goes down in heaven just before the apocalypse and the lord is on his massive throne and he's surrounded by all of those seraphim (not the cherubim, seems lower-class angels weren't invited). and the lamb is removing the seven seals from the scroll one by one, and i came to the verse that says "and when the lamb opened the seventh seal, there was silence in heaven about the space of a half an hour." this line is so bizarre to me because: what the fuck did they all do? just sit there in silence for 30 minutes? that seems so unnecessarily dull.

basically, i want to write a one-act 30-minute real-time play that consists of what goes on between a few of the seraphim, two cheeky homosexuals (based on my brother and me), who are bored out of their minds and trying to entertain themselves while attempting to remain quiet enough so that the lord doesn't notice that they are not actually participating in his oh-so-very-precious half an hour of silence. it would probably consist of mostly whispered dialogue, long periods of unintelligible pantomime, maybe a game of hang-man to kill time, and just them generally trying to contain their own laughter in that sort of "seriously stop i can't even look at you right now or i'll fucking lose it" kind of way that only really happens when you know that you are in a situation where laughter would be absolutely inappropriate.

so it's basically like a contemporary and very american *waiting for godot* during a very boring part of the apocalypse, the proverbial calm before the shit-storm. the play will end with the seraphim cracking up, and all of a sudden, from the heavens (stage center) stephen fry as the lord on a wire is slowly lowered onto the stage from above, holding a pink pistol. he goes to put the seraphim out of their misery but in the process, since he's the type of gay who has clearly never used a gun, fumbles the entire thing. he accidentally kills himself. curtain!

except for the nasty bits, i think religion has a lot to offer art. or maybe it's the other way around.

You twist your flammable ponytail into a question mark as you speed along the Valley cliffs. The shape echoes the curves found in the hills of the raped landscape. You're dying of thirst, searching for water, for Diet Coke, any kind of liquid to assuage your burning Hollywood desires. But it will take hours to get there. And doesn't exist. You drag your hammertoe across the gas pedal. You want a personal glam squad, you want somebody to carefully smudge your eyeliner. You pick the tight rim of skin coating your thumbnail to see if it bleeds. It doesn't anymore.

VICTORIA

Once again, I'm in CVS. I'm lonely. I'm brain-damaged from grief. I find meaning in every casual gesture: the accidental rubbing up against someone's elbow in the painkiller aisle of the pharmacy, as though the elbow has been known before. An elbow from another life, the afterlife of an elbow. The one attached to my body and the one attached to the other body had even known and loved each other once, not the elbows I mean but the bodies. But now when they touch they no longer know each other. Painkilled connection.

On the street, I run into Sasha, who asks me if I want to get a warm beverage. Halfway through my lukewarm coffee at the diner on Moorpark, she asks me about my writing. I respond by ranting, which has been happening a lot recently.

"Only theater people—like Crystal—are worse than the poets" my rant begins to Sasha. "At least poets have the decency to know their place in the world! Theater people are needy, self-aggrandizing, they speak with such gravitas about their rightly diminished profession, as if every one of their projects is something every human needs to reckon with as it contains human truths unavailable to mere plebeians that is so 'urgent' so relevant that we stop whatever we're doing at this moment stop raising our children stop bathing entirely stop life itself and take in their wisdom when in fact what they are selling us are a compendium of known things and their tone-deaf dialogue is likely a mere projection of their own narcissistic pathologies, though to be fair I'm likely disgusted because they inhabit a buried part of myself, because deep down underneath every shrinking violet is a raging exhibitionist just waiting to open their trenchcoat."

Perhaps sensing my desperation, Sasha reaches over the table and grabs my hand.

I am surprised by this intimate turn of events. From a romantic point of view, I am unsavory, not an uninteresting person, not colorless, but typically no woman in their right mind would look at me twice and think I was worth pursuing. Though my face can stop traffic, the stop is north of North Hollywood. But maybe there is a woman for every woman and another woman for every other woman. Maybe not love at first sight but love at second sight, or sightless, the kind of blind love one hears about in the same way one hears about aliens: someone who could both know us and love us. Maybe I could be an erratic housewife to a deaf, blind, and dumb toolmaker. I know how to plant a tree, harvest it too soon, and make it die.

MADELINE

i decided to get out of the house for the first time in a while other than for work and go shopping in chinatown. it was nice to be somewhere other than jail (studio city). i don't mean to complain. things are just weird.

so i went by myself. and for my new womanly figure, i bought a crazy-great short sort of kimono dress that i'm really excited about. i despise the white girl in a kimono with chopsticks in the hair to go out for drinks thing. actually, i think that it looks dreadful, like, why didn't you take the look all the way and put on yellow foundation? so i would never do that, but this kimono is cotton, has a strange, non-traditional pattern, and was actually made for a child so it is shortish dress-length on me, and obviously, i will be pairing it with occidental accessories. so it's not the same thing, i think?

i also bought a samurai sword. but i'm having my doubts now about all of it.

realizing guy responds better to virtual communication even though we're living in the same house, i email him about the sword. it seems he's having his own bout of exoticism. he replied:

Dude, like same.

I had a sex dream last night about a lady Kurdish freedom fighter I saw a pic of who I can't stop thinking about fucking, even though we would be a terrible match for obvious reasons. Anyway in the dream, we're both dressed in 4th century gear, linen tunics

and brown leather sandals (an early Christian vibe).
There's sheepskin everywhere. She's playing a lute or
some shit before I interrupt her demanding she play
some song I like, as a kind of foreplay. She refuses.
Whatever ;(

then my mom came in just as i was figuring out how to
tie the sash around my kimono dress.

"have you heard from guy?" she asked.

"only in email form," i said.

"his door is locked," she said.

i don't see the point in telling our mother that her
son's door has been locked for nearly three years, so
i just say "whatever floats his boat."

On a typical Valley summer evening, the air is desiccated and so are you. You watch the brainiacs traverse an Astroturfed public park, engaging in public acts of air inhalation and improvised sadism. Some throw stones at wild domestic animals, while others take turns spraying one another with essential oils. Children practice depersonalizing themselves on a plastic jungle gym. Nearby a yogini wearing a necklace of dried goat testicles guides a coterie of middle-aged women in spandex through contortions. Coincidentally, a wave of nausea overtakes you. Your nose starts to bleed. You look in your tote bag to see if you have any napkins. You suddenly remember you'd eaten them all a few nights earlier.

VICTORIA

I'm watching Will's DVD of *Point Break* for the second time in a week. In my spring workshop, we discussed a poem a student had written about Keanu Reeves, pioneer of incoherence, matrix of mutism. The words contour his lonely shape on a bench eating a sandwich named "Loneliness." He can go years without talking, even confuse the dead and the living on purpose. His beard is a grief topiary. Like him, I haven't shaved my legs, cut my head-hair, anything since Will died. I'm afraid to shave or cut my locks and have time disappear forever.

✳

Missing them, I email my students about a coyote I saw walk nonchalantly into a Subway in Van Nuys, seeking handouts from its own predators, until Animal Control picked it up and they shared a meatball sub at a booth, predator to predator. Though I tell it half-jokingly, it seems to my students to be the first sign of a deepening psychosis, and the chair of my department orders me to partake in a "restorative session" of my choosing.

So I decide to "restore myself" in a nearby ancient maze designed for ritual purification and soul-cleansing. It's regarded as a passage for the souls of the departed to the spirit world. So I run back and forth across its patterned acreage, shedding all negative emotional states concerning stress, animosity, resentment, exhaustion, frustration, and despair, banishing malevolent ghosts, dancing under the dry heat in a lizard mask and crocs. After five minutes I give up and go search for electrolytes.

Many thanks to my students for instigating such madness.

I don't remember writing this.

✳

Aron emails me back directly, an excerpt from a poem he's been working on:

> *there's an eye eyeing you, nonstop—*
> *you are the eye*
> > *like a hole in a piece of cheese: do you obey it?*
> > > *never mind—keep your eye on the abyss of*
> > > *your choosing*
> > > *on the abyss that responds*
> > > *and loves you*

I write him back: *Thank you for keeping an eye on me.*

✳

I love teaching. I love my genius poetry students. But the technocrats, the faculty crybabies? At this point, the university and the Valley now bear little difference to one another: they're full of obsessive-compulsive minds split from their bodies, testing out their crying jags for maximum impact. All these Overheard in the Valley conversations at the café put our hearts on the line. Today, I saw some teenage girls in the bathroom taking pictures of their stomachs on their phones. They sent them across the world.

MADELINE

it's summer, my least favorite season. it's also guy's least favorite season and back when he left his room, he'd run around saying hostile things like a drunken gay sailor with murky syntax: "beat off!" and "she better not show her ass again in here!" and "get that punk!" it's a dreadful time of year.

around this time last year, i got a letter on my doorstep enclosed in a seabass. the fish guts obscured the message though in some ways the message was clear: pardon the pun, but something fishy was up.

the whole antagonistic gesture put me into a manic state. i tossed the letter in the recycling, brushed my teeth, took my medicine, and while i was slicing some bread to make toast for the fish sandwich i was gonna make with the seabass, i went manic. i was thinking about how fucking great this whole foods organic flax bread is, and what a miracle it is to be alive in a time and place where you can just walk down the street and get bread that tastes like this and it threw me right into the middle of mania.

then i was thinking, i wish the people in my life, particularly the nurses at the psych hospital who insisted that i have an eating disorder because i'm small (okay so i did get rather small*er* in the hospital) could actually come to my house and see me eat this fucking bread then my problems would be entirely solved.

there was one nurse who kept trying to convince me that i was manic. i think she was vaguely aware of the fact that i might be in "a relationship" with another patient, and she probably knew from my chart that i tend to become overly seductive when i am manic. (and come to think of it, on this one, she might have been right.)

but every night, she also tried desperately to convince me that i have an eating disorder, and i would get so mad, like, "can you please focus on helping me with the problems that i actually have instead of inventing fictional ones?" it used to really hurt my feelings and make me angry. of course, i'd complain to my "relationship" about it. "my relationship" would say "that is absolutely ridiculous. if you're losing weight here, it's their fault for putting bacon in everything, and anyway who wants to eat in a fucking hospital? it's depressing as fuck. fuck them." she was wonderful. i wish i could keep her as a reference.

whenever anybody implies that i have an eating problem, i'm just going to be like, "here. call this middle-aged lesbian who believes she caused her brother's death and hears his voice in his head, but who once spent seven consecutive days with me, during which we were only sometimes separated between the hours of 11 pm and 5 am. she can completely put your mind to rest on that matter. never mind the part about her being crazy and maybe killing people and all that." come to think of it, that "relationship" might have been a clue that i'm not entirely straight, which i now know i'm definitely not. dora bought me chopsticks to match my kimono.

anyway today looks like a mostly manic day with impending doom behind it. i'm actually moving around, chain-smoking, shaving the shit out of my legs, turning on and off the coffee pot, and rubbing one out then another and what is scary is i know it isn't going to last. mania is followed by the scariest and most bleak depressions. i long for the days when flax bread would throw me into a frenzied day of productive writing as opposed to this lame jack-off session. i miss those days so, so much.

VICTORIA

I take a few milligrams of speed and start painting my temporary Valley apartment rental a permanent green shade called "climate change." I plan to just do an accent wall in my bedroom, but I get into it, so I paint the entire room, the floor, the ceiling. Then my sneakers, my pill bottles, my nails, and the "delete" key on my laptop.

＊

I re-read Dr. Nicky's last message to me: *Tell me more about the time you overdosed on Lexapro and got trapped on a traffic island for hours.*

＊

As I watch a square-shaped lesbian argue with a checker at the pharmacy over a vat of petroleum jelly, I remember once reading a pop-psychology article that proclaimed that close contact with others reduced prejudice. In the experiments, two sets of two people, two bourgeois and two members of an Amazon tribe, were put in a very small room with only a single bag of Flamin' Hot Cheetos, designed to stimulate the passions. The door was locked. Hours later, when the experimenters came back in, the colonists had been eaten.

＊

William floats above me while I doze with a mountain of vegan cookie crumbs on my Dee Dee Ramone shirt. All of a sudden, he pulls a tube of cream out of his pocket and holds it up to me: *Here, V, try this hand lotion! It smells like croissants and tastes even better!* I grab the lotion and it bursts into flames, singeing the scene to bits.

In the frozen food aisle of Whole Foods in Studio City, you notice that the former child-star's thinning hair is the color of last year, weathered and hayed from brush fires. You wonder if she cuts it herself: nebulous on top and chopped away in patches above the back of her rosacea neck with its marionette creases.

She would almost be homely if she didn't look intelligent: elongated nose and thin mouth, wide-set eyes, a piercing ocean color. Her hollowed frame wasting away in a chinoiserie-patterned dress makes you think of whatever it is you are ashamed of. It's like she can smell your soul's breath.

We've all known her since she was 10 years old. There's nothing she knows about you. That's the only reason you can look her in the eye. She can never return your stare.

Her shoulders are slumped, liquid. When she tries to smile back at you, her eyes flare in their far-away blues.

MADELINE

i felt so weird today at cvs with the christmas music playing despite that its summer waiting for my drugs. part of it was that i still feel lethargic and generally out of it because i spent the day sleeping. i looked horrible… sort of like a corpse wearing a ramones wig.

also the chairs in the waiting area were so soiled and shit-upon that i couldn't bring myself to sit on them, so i positioned all one hundred pounds of my body on the step stool that the employees were using to reach things on the top shelves.

i was situated near the diabetes care section and the tampon aisle, and i saw this couple a little younger than i am, holding hands, buying a blood monitor and then looking at sanitary napkins (quite a bit of blood-shedding between them). they seemed very devoted and would look into each other's eyes to get information about the world and communicate what was on sale and in their budget. and because it's me, all i started thinking about was how i can't even make eye contact with another human being during the sex act. like i'm of the age where i should be able to reasonably handle that sort of level of normal emotional intimacy and not act like a cagey douche. i don't want someone else to love or see me, because then i would actually be a real person to them. i just want to be someone's fond memory and that's all i'm comfortable with. i'm broken. and still waiting for dora to kiss me again.

i keep looking at the butch pharmacist who i'm pretty sure wants to fuck me. she always tries to rush my order of xanax and ritalin to the front of the line, probably thinking i have a night of heavily drugged fucking i need to get to, and probably also thinks i'm rather crazy, and can see the distant deadness in my eyes, and that's why she wants to fuck me. and the fucked-up thing is i kind of like it! but i also realize how deeply abnormal this is. but what can i do? daddy and mommy had their issues. i lie in the bed they made.

VICTORIA

I've dreamed I was a star in the sky, I've dreamed I was sand on a beach, but the sand was beating hearts, I've dreamed I was a pretty strangled waitress. I've dreamed I was my mother, I've dreamed I was her mother and my father, I've dreamed my ex's mother was a plastic surgeon and she gave me a boob job, a perfect C. I've never dreamed that I am or was myself.

✳

I used to have so many friends. There was the sweet one with dark hair who was always on the verge of mortal dread. There was the communist candy-lover. There was the one outlined in black ink filled in with bright colors. There was the one who was always on the margins of the page, nostalgic for old technology. There was the one who loved Sid Vicious and hated the Yugoslav new wave. There was the Turkish poet. I don't know where we all went.

✳

I hate summer. Almost as much as Will hated summer. I never saw my brother with his shirt off, even in a pool. He had an almost pathological fear of UV rays, long July days, happy children in bathing suits. So, it's ironic he's being memorialized in summer, the height of Sun Damage Season. Thanks to our childhood, I'm lacquered by the sun, decoupaged with freckles and sun spots. I mean, at a certain point, surviving life gracefully becomes a real achievement. I think this just as I see my mother drink out of a boot flask in the shape of a shark, bringing the alcohol to her marked, lined face.

Behind her, I see a shrine my mother has erected in my brother's honor. I'm normally the dude in the corner of the room too overwhelmed to cross a room, but today I'm floating with ease as I go up to the shrine. My mom placed one of the framed photographs that was taken in honor of our birth, a Madonna and Child with our mother and us as infants set against a backdrop of a California orange grove. The whole humiliating event took place at Sears in North Hollywood.

I notice recently deposited bird-shit on the photo, humorously spoiling my mother's '80s-era shoulder-padded suit. I feel the tragedy of all of us encapsulated in nature's little artistic gesture. I want to share this sublime moment with someone and suddenly have a sense for the first time since my brother's death that something has been missing: him.

MADELINE

literally my only hope is with my psychiatrist. i feel like, if anyone can save me, can make my life tolerable again, it's him.

but our relationship does concern me because i know that all of my fears about erotic transference are completely valid. i do tend to be seductive with dr. nicky when i'm in one of my moods, but to my credit, i have enough self-awareness to stop it when it gets too hot between us.

like when i was in the hospital, he and i used to have our daily meetings in my room. one time, during my first stay, i just happened to be sort of lying on my bed, on my side, with my feet near the pillow, and my head near the end of the bed where he was sitting. it was totally innocent. i was talking about how much i can talk my brains out and how rapidly i tend to move when i'm super manic and that i find that i'm very polarizing: people either find it exciting or endearing or annoying and unbearable. and the doc said, "well, i like you very much." and i kind of rolled over, and looked at him upside down, and said "be careful. you know i have problems with impulse control." he kind of laughed and said something like, "are you just being cheeky, or do i need to up your lithium?" i immediately hit myself on the head to distract both of us. it likely made me appear crazier but it worked.

i have to try to stop that from happening in the first place though because i need to keep the doc and because there is just something wrong with my mind. i mean, i don't think i want to try to seduce my psychiatrist?!

i confide in guy about it and he texts me:

Makes sense: Moon-Mars in Scorpio and Mercury-Jupiter in Leo (this doesn't happen often), forming two sets.

I'm wondering if global affairs will get even more distressing, and I hope not. But this is, frankly, dour astro-news.

Fixed squares are nasty and Mars is not in the mood to fuck around right now. Not in that sign.

The conjunction is just going to blow hot air around and have people be more zealous.

Pay attention to "cease-fires" in the news and how they unfold, or collapse.

People acting too heavily on impulse/misinformation. Bloodlust. Road-rage. Sexuality.

Just speculations here.

The zombies cross Ventura Blvd in clean diagonal lines. You queue up for no apparent reason. You don't know if you're waiting for frozen yogurt or cryotherapy or for the Sprinkles Cupcake Yoga Brunch at the Surgery Bar Powered by Porn. It doesn't matter. You begin to identify as queer and straight. You begin to suspect you're actually your own twin. You are a piece of art capable of criticizing itself, endlessly passing back and forth between your own hands a doll's teacup filled with human tears.

VICTORIA

I wake up in a panic shouting out loud: "Panic is ancestral!" I wonder if waking up and saying it aloud is also ancestral.

✳

What's strange is that we go on after someone dies. But stranger still as a twin, sharing real estate in the same womb at the same time as you. Now one face turned toward reality, the other face turned toward the dream. One light and one dark, a dark horse and its shadow, a small jockey and a ghost rider. Hm. Maybe I'm not going on at all.

✳

Amongst the greatest failures, the failure to commit suicide must be up there among the most shameful. Suicide is an act of immortality, a desire to live beyond the grave, beyond the limits imposed upon a life, like this bit of corn clinging to my blouse begging to be tossed or befriended.

My spell-check keeps telling me there's no one way to write "suicideation." Why can't god make it easy for me?

✳

I impulsively get a nose piercing. As I look in the mirror at the blood running down my cheek, I also notice that my hair's been dyed an awful shade of pink. I've clearly regressed. But more to the point, I need to stop doing this stuff at home.

✳

Back at the diner on Moorpark, I tell Sasha that my mother accused me of "mental endangerment" and "brain gardening" and called me a "sociopath entrepreneur," even though I was just dropping off a roast chicken for dinner. Later, she hugged me and said I was a perfect daughter.

"Look," Sasha says. "I love Skyla, but she can't be a mother right now. Not to be so basic and woo-woo, but you need to be a mother to your inner child. It's time for you to parent yourself."

"I don't know if I'm ready," I say. "I just wish Will was here. I need a father figure," I say, choking back tears.

✳

Looking at a photo of myself as a child, naked and hosing a lawn that doesn't seem to exist, I think: "She's just so vulnerable, so child-like, my instinct is to hold her and want to protect her." I wonder if I am on the spectrum. I'm about to snort Ambien with a Twizzler to stop feeling anything. Instead, I decide to text Will:

I start:

It's so lonely here. Come back.

He writes:

I can't ever return. I'm so sorry, V. I would have to relearn everything all over like a dumb baby.

MADELINE

i just had a terrible incident with a pimple i just couldn't accept on my face and took the liberty of popping it. now, i normally don't have trouble maintaining my composure in the face of sanguine humour (or blood, if one is to believe in modern medicine), and yet to my own surprise, when a single drop of blood appeared at the end of the bursting cyst, i swooned like a maiden, and took to the floor before gravity did it for me. i kept the bathmat over me for warmth for a good 15 minutes before fully regaining consciousness. was i stoned at the time? does it matter?

i tell guy about my lady woes and also confess to having a lady crush.

guy writes me:

> *Dude time to step away from the snacks! Been reading the news. Jesus, is everything and everyone crazy? A comet laden with Thorazine needs to smash into this planet.*

speaking of drugs i am in such a weed trance right now it's unbelievable (see pimple snafu). it seems to work exceedingly well with my new medication. the only problem is, it makes me hyper focused and a little socially loose. for example earlier today i made a little video inspired by dora. last night she stopped by whole foods because she supposedly ran out of flax seeds and we started talking about morrissey versus the smiths in the bulk aisle.

so anyway earlier today i thought i was being very clever when i drove up to mulholland singing morrissey then took out my camera and starting shooting a video of trees and smog. and i literally have no idea why other than drugs. but the worst of it is that i emailed the video to dora (!) with the subject line *self-portrait for you*. she hasn't replied and i have this sick, shameful feeling, the kind you get when you make a massive social faux pas. like when you take a risk, and it then suddenly occurs to you that there's a reason no one has ever sent you a video of themself singing just for you.

guy follows up:

> *Dude I'll tell you what: tomorrow we can watch this new DVD edition of Holy Mountain I copped. I know how much you fucking love the toads versus iguanas reenactment of the Crusades. and I'll give you half a Vicodin for the lady stuff and half to take to your room when your self-esteem goes to shit again. LOVE YOU.*

VICTORIA

When I heard my brother died, I gathered up all the photographs I had of him and drew mustaches on them. I don't know what that was about.

※

The last time I took ketamine I had an uncanny moment while I was reading *American Psycho* and was certain I had written it, horrified but also lavishing myself with obscene praise, the kind of praise rarely observed outside of a gay bathhouse, until the spell broke and realized: I was mortal, I was back in the Valley, and I was possibly turning into another person.

※

Ketamine? I ask into the mirror. No, honey, it's Death that's the ultimate form of dissociation.

※

And what are drugs and what is Time itself but substitutions for Reality? I miss it, reality. Often, I awaken to find myself idle and beached alone amidst a traffic stream of boxy cars and meridian slashes, where the pavement meets the beach, staring at an ancient road sign admonishing me, DEAD END. I have missed the harmony that connects the beginning to this weird end. Have I outlived myself? There is no synchronization of events, no causality, just me melting into sizzling butter on a traffic island, surrounded by no mourners. Just those who would toss me back into the sea, making a sound so unworldly that I would drive the seagulls around me to commit suicide.

It's rare I get fucked-up enough to end up in the neighbor's swimming pool.

✳

I can't sleep and I can't write, so I take myself to CVS for lunch and Sudafed. They're playing "Last Christmas" by George Michael except in my head I keep saying "Boy George" and also, it's summer.

A mob of thrilled teenagers buying xanthan gum in bulk whisper to themselves that I'm a vampire, a loser, Winona Ryder. Like my chocolate gasoline drink, their mixture of admiration and disgust keeps me going. Every place has its own delicate ecosystem.

I run through the store snatching energy drinks and protein bricks and thinking of the amount of writing I have begun, only to tear it up or toss it in the incinerator because my brother, deceased, has rudely shown up in the middle of my process.

These things cannot be enumerated. Still, maybe I will try with a piece of writing that I would call "men" after the Man Ray photograph "Waking Dream Séance," where a group of men hover over a woman, a common theme though, in this case, the woman is Simone Breton, André Breton's wife, essentially a vessel through which the dreams of the Surrealists are transcribed onto paper, so she is a stenographer of dada personality disorder, having no dreams of her own, just a child muse, a weird little child-woman doll, or even worse, like Breton's Nadja, who's literally a Ouija board mistaken for the narrator's mistress, where the "Who am I?" of masculine subjectivity meets the "Put your fingers on me and slide them around until you find yourself" of feminine objectivity, alterity that keeps the species running on all cylinders, even in the case of homos.

Sasha appears out of nowhere to save me from Theory. She tells me that Morrissey once said about James Dean: "He was incredibly miserable and obviously doomed. People who feel this are quite special."

Studio City mourns all these deaths at once, and you fall in love with an older love that's a memory. After many years of sleeping, you walk down Moorpark Drive near the Italian restaurant, Vitello's, that used to be an Italian restaurant across the street also named Vitello's, not quite sleeping, nearly awake just before you die again looking inside from outside at someone's plate of bad spaghetti. You listen for your own lonely heartbeat amid an operatic silence. A washed-up celebrity, a silent star, whose saucy lips move across a restaurant-length distance, disappears supernaturally into the Santa Anas sweeping through lunch. That beautiful image will forever be emblazoned onto your heart's sleeve.

MADELINE

having a crush on someone or having someone like you is one of the best feelings in the world. especially when it is new, or in my case, if you are particularly fucked-up, *only* if it is new. i'm so excited that my nightly sleeping pills aren't conking me out, so it *must* (*really into italics today*) be bad. because my nightly cocktail is like a bucket of horse tranquilizers for the average person and beyond enough to put down the average horse unless said horse happened to have a massive crush on another horse.

i guess what i'm trying to say is that i'm cautiously optimistic but allowing myself the strange mixture of joy/fear/indigestion/shadow theater/horse dressage/ anorexia/incest taboo that these types of situations inevitably conjure is not necessarily a bad thing. not being able to focus on anything or get anything done for a while can certainly be frustrating but is it really going to cause any damage to speak of in the long run? this is one of the few good feelings in life's over-running cache of shit emotions. i'm gonna enjoy it while it lasts because soon enough me and my lover will be fighting and smothering each other and hurting each other's feelings.

so anyway dora visited me yesterday at whole foods where i was taking an unhealthy smoke break out back. moody and mysterious, she approached me in the alley by the tossed-away organic fruit carcasses as i was taking a cigarette into my mouth. she said something off-color about the sex life of a banana that managed to be complex, psychological, and botanical all once, something about how bananas are sterile and haven't had sex in thousands of years. and she saw my exposed forearm and commented on my beckett tattoo. "yeah, 'so it goes'— but where?" she said. and i'm so desperate and reckless it practically made me cum. i stubbed out my cigarette and hysterically said something to the effect of: "why don't we just fuck or something?" and then she said: "oh, wow you really know how to demystify things, don't you?" we both agreed it was probably not the best idea to have sex in an alleyway with the stench of rotting fruit and old cigarette butts. she's like the cross-dressing boy who seduces orlando and fucks him up a little. i hope i don't get pregnant.

i email guy about my romantic awakening, and guy writes me back:

> Getting a boyfriend or girlfriend (?!) is good to have on the "to do" list. but my (ugh, cough) philosophy on that is that it just might happen when it happens and forcing stuff like that (not that u r) tends to produce uncomfortable/unnecessary situations/interactions. take it from me, lol. For real. I've been checking into that motel on and off the past few months and I've noticed it's largely been a way to avoid dealing with the real.

later i dream that my father is on a small stage masturbating. as the only members of the audience, my brother and i are stuck watching it. i'm not sure what i was dreaming of when i woke up, but i was crying with that song about samson and delilah by regina spektor playing over and over in my head. "you are my sweetest downfall. i loved you first." but who was i thinking of? i don't even know. i want to think it's dora, but i think it's my father.

today my sweetest downfall/dora came into whole foods again as i was stacking loose sacks of ground flaxseed.

"hey there, stranger," she said. i went to speak but instead sneezed at her as flaxseed shards went up my nostril.

"so you're huffing flax now?" she joked.

"hey, valley life is rough," i badly joked back.

"well, i don't want to worry about you when i'm gone," she said. "i'm headed to san francisco. visit friends, stare at the bay, breathe in air that's not smoggy. i just need to get out of town for a bit. the valley can feel really small sometimes, you know? even though you make it much bigger, despite your small stature." she smiled at me and i missed her already.

"maybe we can be penpals?" i said, more vulnerable than i had meant to be.

"of course we can and we will. i'll miss you, you know," she said to me, kissing me on the cheek.

i wanted to say, "i'll miss you more." instead, i rang her up for groceries and gave her my employee discount.

VICTORIA

When Will and I started our punk band, well past the point of punk, I suggested we call ourselves Digging Graves, because we appreciated the dual meaning of digging, in the sense of breaking ground with a shovel and also liking. Aquapuke won over in the end.

I knew we were in trouble when I broke out the Smiths' "The Queen is Dead" and began making an "I know it's over" drawing where our mother and Will are standing over my open grave in the middle of the desert and my brother is on all fours with a bandana on his head and sunglasses blowing desert dirt onto me and there is a caption that says "Mother, I can feel the soil falling over my head."

Will suggested we go to the desert and try to shoot the scene. Will and I had tried to have a band before, called "Pet Seabass" after the Monty Python "fish license" sketch where Praline tries to get a license for his pet halibut. It was also an inside joke about how an ex-girlfriend once tossed a dead seabass on my doorstep.

We had essentially been a double act since birth, adopting Tolstoy's "All happy families are alike, every unhappy family is unhappy in its own way" as our sort of slogan. Except it wasn't an act and we weren't fictional Russians.

I realized I couldn't be in a band for the same reason I couldn't be in a relationship. I was shit at it. I didn't need Will and he didn't need me. I needed to be on my own, personally and creatively.

So that day, I went back to writing a dialogue between me and a mannequin.

MADELINE

re: my snatch, i hadn't heard from dora in a few days so i stupidly had a meaningless one-nighter with a videographer for an electronic band that dresses in space suits. i've come to the conclusion that i am not at all a fan of anything ribbed. especially when it is all that i have available and have to continue to use it through several rounds of extended fucking. i don't know anything about "barbed." that just sounds scary and makes me think of pamela anderson. i'm not sure it is possible to chafe in an area that is generally moist, so maybe raw is a better word. all jokes about popsicles and icicles aside, it might actually be an ice situation. i told my gentleman caller it feels like i've been raped by a cheese grater, which is not only painful, but also offends my vegan sensibilities. he said that maybe it wouldn't be so bad if i imagined the cheese was a "so delicious" product. but really it isn't the ribbed condom and chafing that worries me. it's what that contains, so to speak. it's that i continue to feel nothing when i fuck guys, like i'm dead inside, like there's a reason i'm a slut for them.

i asked guy if he thought there was sexually something wrong with me and he didn't think it was that big of a deal.

Dude, chill the fuck out. YOU ARE FINE.

I don't know why I didn't start cleaning houses, years ago. I told you I put an ad in Craigslist, right? "In search of a scruffy otter for regular house cleaning?

I'm your man! Have a fantastically clean house by a friendly beard in a jock."
I had my first gig last night. Nothing sinister happened.
I made $200 in 4 hours. Mind=blown.

guy is on his own strange trip. so i think about dora. i think of her pouty mouth, her bangs, her freckled eyes, stripping away her mystery.

VICTORIA

My mother's new nurse calls to tell me that the other day and in fact many other days recently, my mother has found herself monologuing to a lampshade.

✳

I go to check on my mom and find her arranging Scrabble pieces on the kitchen table. When I ask her why there is a blow-up Santa Claus on the lawn even though it is summer, she arranges the Scrabble pieces to spell out "i s a r r y ."

She then gets up and puts on a Bob Marley record, which I've never seen before (neither the player nor the record). She tells me, going in and out of patois, "When I play Bob, the birds make U-turns in my direction, all the men in town make a beeline toward me, the world opens itself up. *You* should try it. *Yu welkom. Now lef mi alone.*"

Turns out the new nurse has been teaching my mother patois to help her with her memory. Unfortunately, my mom now sounds less demented but more like a pothead, which I suppose is a sort of progress.

On my way out, I notice Santa is now deflated and wet from the sprinklers. He looks like he's had one too many. He looks at peace and I am insanely jealous.

✳

I just remembered last Christmas I did ketamine with Dr. Nicky. We talked about our mothers, then watched *Xanadu* on a giant leather couch. I remember saying to him very slowly, "This is a perfect film."

MADELINE

dora has literally lifted me temporarily out of the darkness for the first time in nearly twenty four hours. i got an email from her from san francisco. it was just what i needed. it was sweet and weird and rambling, and it made me remember why i liked her so much. she seems to operate in her own alternate world, and there is no place for sadness there. only excessive use of punctuation. who needs sadness when you can have seven question marks???????

NUDITY IS NOT A CRIME = Most amazing bumper sticker I have ever seen???????
I love San Fran.

I'm staying in a lesbian commune and it's a great place if you need a place to stay in the city. And we live across the street from magnificence: there is a lady across the street with three Boston terriers. She has two separate vehicles for them and has them pull her along on her walks! One is a standing scooter, and one is a straight-up chariot.
Yes, terrier chariot. It's like a sitting cart like they have behind those weird trotting horse races. I gotta get a pic for you. She's my hero!!

Anyway, thank you for giving me your email address. I've been thinking of you and I wanted to tell you that.

xx Dora

i'm so grateful for dora buffering me against my home life. i will say mom actually tried to make a lovely dinner for just the two of us tonight. but there were ingredients were missing or off: the pasta was half-cooked, the salad didn't have dressing, there were a handful of raisins on a plate. she didn't touch anything, and when i tried to talk to her she just started staring out the window at the wild parrot who sometimes visits us. i said "mom?" and she didn't answer. then called her by her name, "celine?" but she didn't respond. she didn't seem to recognize my voice.

VICTORIA

I frequently go to the public reading room in the Studio City library, which doesn't even exist. I consult the microfiche, poring over obituary notices from 100 years ago, from 25 years ago, news of deaths that happened before I was born and just after I had died, news of a celebrity death of an actress who had been rumored to be dead long before her actual death, notes upon the passage of her life into the afterlife of this record. And news of my brother's death, giving me reassurance that it wasn't in fact I who had committed suicide after all. Though occasionally I do find my name listed among the dead right after Jayne Mansfield's vehicular death, shearing her wig into a projectile vaulting off her head, the body glaring white becoming a ghost because someone had wished her home.

*

I've taken to wandering nightly along dilapidated buildings undergoing facelifts. The Valley is a region that has largely outlived its purpose, at the dead-end of creation, Camelot's shadow. The cars abandoned along the street bear the marks of their owners: a basket full of taco shells, costume jewelry in a jar, a yellow umbrella with the words "Pray for Rain," a deflated basketball in a passenger's seat flirting with sentience. At the end of the static funeral procession, I see an old cowboy horse, harnessed and riderless, carrying a hangman's rope in its mouth, splotched with nakedness and gray chin hairs. He stares at me with a hanging head, dark eyes leaking smog.

He bears the look of my grandmother just before she passed away. She was wearing a half-death mask in her bed surrounded by a fort of faded-floral throw pillows, the King James Bible, and a bottle of cheap gin filled with olive pimentos, as my mother and I stood over her, my mother at the time drugged out of her mind into callousness for she felt abandoned by her mother and chose this very moment to express her woundedness, muttering to no one, "Only someone so weak would die so dumbly."

"What are you staring at, that donkey statue???" asks Sasha, standing facing me, punctuating my nightmare. "If you stare any longer, you're gonna get foot and mouth disease and that shit eats holes in your brain and stuff."

"Did you know poets are twenty times more likely than anyone else to end up in an asylum?" I ask.

Sasha tenderly tugs at the sleeve of my black "Girl-friend in a Coma" T-shirt. "Oh honey, we have to go shopping and get you out of your 'sad' costume," she tells me.

You stare somewhere between the sky and the clown-colored, clown-shaped and clowning Circus Liquor sign that dominates the field of vision against the Santa Susana Mountains.

You look for a cigarette, for caustic crumbs of tobacco, going so far as to rummage through trash bins for odds and ends, taping them together, then smoking the giant phallus to ashes.

In the parking lot, you throw stones at pigeons and realize you weren't actually hired for the writing job, which explains why you haven't been paid.

Surveying the environment, you realize most of the green stays locked in the palm trees and the rest of the Valley is scorched earth. But the liquor store clown mascot is a bright hemorrhaging of blue and red, an intricate work of toxic waterways and toxic gasses, held up to the sky in its contours of smirks, held up for the sky to listen.

You're there only to bring it all down.

MADELINE

studio city is so boring and predictable and obvious: juice bars, tensionless architecture, high-impact aerobics. i'm craving novelty. thank god dora isn't boring. she emails me *again* (!) from san francisco:

> *Hi I thought of you while looking for cotton panties today, and read a 5-star review of Highlegs on Amazon: "Perfect design & luxury cotton feel. Practical & amazingly comfortable. After these, nothing else will compare. Quite pretty, but could be a touch more feminine with a bow or lace trim. If they did more colors than black or white I would want them all. Sizes seem accurate. Guess women will also like them." Love the gender-bending twist at the end!*

> *Anyway, I thought of you when I read that. I hope you haven't encountered any insecticide since we last corresponded—didn't you say you were rereading Kafka? In any event, I am getting out of San Fran just in time. I have never in my life seen so many dramatic encounters/weirdnesses/people acting unhinged over the course of a week. I tried to keep my distance by floating in the tub on an inflatable dragon for the most part, but I did have to leave the bathroom on occasion to eat and sleep. Most unfortunate.*

> *I miss you.*
> *xx Dora*

my mom came into my room with an oval portrait of a dog and puppy she had been working on (she seems to spend all her time painting these days). "this schnauzer and her puppy is a portrait of us as newborn baby and newborn mama," she told me.

i stared at the sad-eyed schnauzers and then at my mom's smeared eye makeup. i couldn't tell any of our eyes apart.

VICTORIA

Back at Skyla's I feel hot and wild and need air conditioning. I go inside to take respite in my favorite room, into Will's bedroom, a museum filled with his books—on astrology, cosmography, phrenology, taxidermy, Iggy Pop, puppies of the world—and his eyeglasses, frozen in time. Despite my mother's tendency to clean frenziedly, absolving herself of the guilt of merely existing through excessive dusting and burning of unwanted clothing, she somehow couldn't allow my brother's bedroom to be gutted, as though evacuating that would be a sin against the dead, including her mother, my grandmother, that famous obsessive-compulsive. In my brother's safe room, I can think more clearly. Everything feels staged and fake and unreal. I can imagine a playbill taking us through the various acts of derangement. My brother, if he were alive, would have died on the spot. He used to call his bedroom the Captain's Cabin after the bar he frequented on Victory Boulevard, boulevard of small victories, the only place where he could be alone.

*

For many years after our father left us for Italy and homoerotic adventures, I would sometimes fall into these depressive, semi-hysterical states of mind. I would get chest pains and have to lie down and cry because it felt like someone had violently removed a part of me without my permission. Will was the person I would call to talk through panicked, sad, child-like responses to breakups or getting a flat tire on the 101, or not understanding a 401k.

Now, falling into a fit of depression is a way to conjure him. To the extent I regress, I'm able to make him come back. Back to where we're still best friends and our lives exist in parallel.

＊

I email Aron and it bounces back. *This email address no longer exists.*

MADELINE

although it's only just midday and i only just woke up i'm marking an x on my calendar, hoping to will it into being over, even though i have no future to look forward to. i think it should be mentioned that my sanity is a little shaky. the thought occurred to me that, if one is to believe berkeley and his little obsession with immaterialism, there are many, many days where i simply do not exist. and then if one is to believe the carpenters: "loneliness is such a sad affair."

every day all i have to look forward to is going to yoga before my shift. that's my only reason to get up in the morning. after class i just lie there until the next class comes and think "when is this going to be over?" clearly, i no longer want to live, but i've learned my lesson with the suicide thing. i've learned that it is very difficult to get right, and i don't want to end up in some shit hospital again.

i email my brother about not having a future, having no purpose in life, nothing to distract me from the insanity of living (dora is still in san francisco), hoping he can bring me out of it. he responds with:

Dude, look, anything can happen. Imagine a future as a wasteland where extremists rule and gays are hunted (like in Running Man, that Schwarzenegger movie) by a 7th century looking vice squad. Gays and lesbians would adopt extra-sensory perceptions and become super-tough replicants.

An all-female brigade of poets named after you would feature heavily in this armed existential desert conflict of the future replete with astrological underpinnings.

Luckily this isn't going to happen. Either way, chill out, you'll be FINE!

he has a way of soothing me.

VICTORIA

My mom taught junior high art history. She didn't believe in absolute knowledge and regarded textbooks as ideological tools of oppression. Instead, she would put out modeling clay and instruct us to sculpt our ideas or the noses of famous muses. Some parents complained, and one day, mom wasn't asked to come back. I remember her pulling us out of school that day, yelling at the principal "Only boring children like routine! Give them their fentanyl lollipops!"

She took us to the Beverly Garland Hotel to take a dip in the pool, which they usually let us do because my mom also worked part-time as an hors d'oeuvres maker at the Hotel's restaurant, Baby Garland. My mom ordered us all Shirley Temples, and suggested we imagine ourselves in a different life, out of the Valley, a life of easy glamor.

I remember how sunshine splashed on the surface of the pool, and peonies, garlands of peonies cut to fit vases on small tables, and the maraschino soda I drank like champagne because at the time we thought death could be glamorous, too. These pleasure cocktails were what William and I toasted to, no guilt chasers, we ran around like bandits, losing our goddamn minds before the audience of one. "Best Actress, Best Actor, Best Original Screenplay!" said mom. And she dove into the pool wearing her work dress, sunglasses, shoes, then quickly emerged with smeared lipstick.

Yes, I had encroaching lesbian desires of combing our teenage neighbor's long hair into ribbons of gold, parting the strands with my teeth, but I loved my brother and my mother more than anything. We had our weird matrimony dreams because the world at the time had to be imaginary. We three would be married at our favorite diner, DeMorgue's, and we would invite everyone, including my grandmother's desert cactus she called Sylvia, the California family of quail that lived nearby, the wily coyote that would come up to our fence looking for a morsel of my mother's famous bean dip, the moon that would dress up as the sun, the LA River that would reverse its course and flow into the backyard, and Diana our beloved waitress at our favorite diner, who would come bearing buttered pancakes, after hanging a sign on the diner's window announcing: "We're out to lunch."

MADELINE

i've been living like a disgusting slob, a bachelor. if i don't find more work soon i might just migrate from pasta with jarred sauce to spaghettios. i've been wandering the apartment in jean cut-offs and an old wife-beater with holes in it. i've given up on bathing unless there's a definite possibility someone might go down on me. and even then, what does washing my hair have to do with it? mostly i listen to jeff buckley and draw rabbits that look like stephanie. it's disgusting.

dora is still in san fran so mostly i'm alone. and the problem with being alone all the time when you're especially weird is you become so isolated in your own strange thoughts that they start to take on a life of their own. i reckon the idea of finding another person who has equally strange and complementary thoughts somehow makes the whole situation less isolating. i used to feel like that with guy.

there's something wrong with me that i can't even cry at actual, human stuff. i was sad but didn't shed a single tear when my father left. somehow though i did, however, cry when jeff buckley died and when elliott smith died, and i certainly didn't "know" them. and i remember being really sad when amy winehouse died, but that's it. i'll cry for days when nick cave goes. sometimes i wonder if i'll cry if my brother goes before i do. it's just weird crying for someone you don't know anymore. it's like mourning the loss of an idea you once had. actually, it is exactly that.

VICTORIA

I zone out on my new fake-velvet, curved sectional couch like I'm falling in love, or I'm gonna fuck it. But really how wonderful it would be to love something that feels nothing—how happy it must be to have no emotions, to just sit on the floor, be cute and functional, and never experience pain or suffering!

✳

Sasha suggested I try out haiku, saying I need more constraint in my life:

too depressed to fuck
no interest in showering
golden/otherwise

hand sanitizer
endure wellbutrin funhouse
bony lady sad

i wrote about her
that time i used a strap-on
gayest poem ever

blowing ur brains out
lobotomy head leaves
u dumber than u came

✳

I've collected old books, words, used kitchen equipment. I've let fresh flowers dry in their vases and kept them there. I've kept a golden lock of my childhood dog's hair in a plastic baggie near my pillow. Hopefully, one day my life's purpose will be revealed to me. Hopefully, it's before I'm dead.

＊

I dreamed I was emptying all the vases for my brother's memorial into the manmade pond at the Sportsman's Lodge. Sasha was helping me, but then we got bored and went to the nearby Erewhon to get a smoothie made with Gwyneth Paltrow's tears. The flowers in the vases were cartoonish and plastic, their faces like bloated little American Girl Dolls. We used to come here as kids and our grandmother would toss breadcrumbs into the pond to attract the geese, who would then psychotically chase us away. I panned the area for loose geese and realized I was in my grandmother's old apartment on Moorpark, staring at her doll collection, her little jade trees in little pots, her chipped teacups standing along the windowsill, catching and refracting light onto a framed poster of a *Starry Night* from a Van Gogh exhibit from 1989, a flat sky, a whirlpool of death, the moon lifting awkwardly off the top, and a church that seems plucked from Halloween waits for the Santa Anas to finish everything off. It's so corny, I think, but the world loves it and so did she. Suddenly, the front door to the apartment closes from the wind, the sound loud enough to make the entire thing entirely plausible.

＊

But now I'm feeling much better on account of an old friend: self-prescribed amphetamines. Also, a new friend: Sasha.

MADELINE

sometimes i am struck with this overwhelming feeling of homesickness, like the kind you have as a kid when you're shipped off to sleep-away camp, or even just dropped off at school in the morning when you secretly want to stay home with mom and bake cookies (this is someone else's childhood entirely, but you get the drift), just some weird longing to return from where you came." it will happen out of nowhere, i'll just be going about my business, and suddenly i am overtaken by the desire to go home. only, i live here, and this is home, and if it is not, then i have no idea what i am longing for because this is certainly the closest thing i've got.

guy tells me:
Dude, everyone's moon has issues. A planet with no issues is a boring planet belonging to a boring person.

true, but maybe boring's better than batshit.

VICTORIA

My mother seems to be losing an argument with a person she insists is called Mrs. Dickson and wants me to call the cops. She is wary of what seems to be a permanent intruder in a temporary world. My mother is certainly not the person she had been nor is Mrs. Dickson, who my mother is now calling Mrs. Blixon. It is an established piece of reality that my mother killed her former self years ago and that it is this self, this former self, who follows my mother around, haunting the living shit out of her, as she wants to remain dead. There is no room for this former self nor for Mrs. Dixon-Blintzen, either, as my mother is now calling her, in the inn, in this theater set, where everyone's SAG card had been revoked, no more extras, everything has changed, the studio system is now a ghost town. Maybe all that occurs is whatever the next thing is that happens. Fuck it. I may as well try to interview the Pacific.

✳

In the pharmacy aisles, I stare at generic painkillers, out-of-vogue vitamins, cheap Chardonnays, knock-off perfumes, all gathering dust and at the lowest point in their careers, nearing the end even if people don't want to admit it, abandoning abandonment.

✳

Another mother story (she likes to talk to animals): "She's the most beautiful cactus I've ever seen!" my mother says to a spiky-haired dog with blind-brown cataracts. Luckily, the dog has mastered the art of deadpan and doesn't even budge when my mom pokes its body seeking out thorns. I wonder if it's the color, the scent, the affect, what exact line of associations sends Skyla into a fit of giggling, asking the dog's alarmed owner, "She's so friendly! How often do you water her?"

MADELINE

at work today i take advantage of my employee discount and excitedly zone out on a piece of flax bread in the break room thinking about all-female-poet police brigades. i'm distracted by this anarchist possibility, and i keep getting in trouble for not being on the floor, as i'm supposed to be helping get people "pumped up" for Organic College Month. my manager made up a mood board for what he wanted the store to look like in celebration, but my coworkers and i couldn't make heads or tails of it. it was basically just a bunch of stock photos of college idiots screaming and cheering in their pennant-covered dorm rooms. my manager drew pictures of fruit all over, and on a post-it note pasted to the board he wrote "fill their backpack!" but actually it said "back-back!" in the end we handed out miniature backpacks of electrolytes to every customer who made a vegetable purchase of more than thirty dollars.

one of those customers was dora. she's back (back) from san francisco! and i swear over the month or so she has been gone, she has magically turned into fucking lady godiva. her hair is so long that she wears it in a massive, thick knot at the nape of her neck. it's not even a massive top-knot! it's a massive low-knot! that shit must be down to her mid-back, but how on earth is that possible? i swear her hair was only shaggy-type length not too long ago. it wasn't even to her chin! how?! i thought maybe she was participating in medical experiments or something.

so i asked her where she'd been and said something like "your hair looks longer than when i last saw you, did you have it extended?" and she laughed and didn't even flinch at the most awkward thing i have ever said to anyone. instead, she asked me on a date.

You stop for what you thought would be a year in the Valley, spending your savings on costumes purchased at the mall, buying everything in sight—velvet dress, an ashen wig, black-gloved hands—changing your name to Boneheart, changing your look from head to toe, developing an accent, casualizing your language, attending your own funeral at the Calabasas pet cemetery, burying your taxidermized spirit animal, a peacock with a massive cock, who might have been your prince, feathering your hands and cheeks, except that he's invisible, so you stand alone, out of your mind and out of your heart against a background of oil slicks and thick smog. No one notices you.

VICTORIA

My mom has been washed out to sea, an unhappy clam shellacked, barnacled baby. It's easier to believe that my twin who has died is alive than it is to believe my mother is alive and not dead, or for that matter myself. My twin stopped dreaming at the end and I wonder do I dream through him or does he dream through me? *What?!* is my constant message to myself.

✳

My mom emerges from the house, having a great sense of the theatrical, and goes screaming right into a pack of power-walkers.

✳

My brother and Skyla were tethered at the umbilical cord even into his adulthood, and they would sometimes even dress alike, which was not just comic, but off-putting, not just weird, but borderline repellent. Mom and he liked to taunt me that I was a "loser-genius," shouting at me until I would throw a book at the wall and sink into a medically significant depressive episode, ruminating on the extraordinary mediocrity of human beings, especially myself, which led to a lifelong addiction to diplomas, where my favorite words became *Beckett*, *Paris*, *psychoanalysis*, *cockblocking riding jerky*, *the frozen food imaginary*, *the fluid pigments of the body*, a self-righteousness knowledge tsunami pouring forth like exorcist's vomit.

✳

One day when we were teenagers, Will disappeared, and mom was driving home late at night. Our mother could fall asleep anywhere—at a disco party, at a child's christening, during divorce proceedings—her head rolling around her thin neck, all caused by clogged sinuses we learned years later, an especially stuffy nose, which interrupted her sleep patterns and made her generally demented. We lived up the road from an assisted living home just off Ventura Blvd, called A Place for Her, where little old ladies would sit outside in their lawn chairs, and wave to the cars driving by, yelling hellos and goodbyes. That night, all the ladies were supposed to be asleep, but one got loose and ran into the street. And mom, driving slowly but erratically, clipped her, knocking her to the ground. She was fine and would tell the story until she died years later in her sleep, but mom totaled the car when she hit the neighbor's lawn sculpture of an eighteenth-century celebrity holding a baseball bat. Later she wrote an apology letter to the lady she clipped, who by this time was in another state of mind. Mom apologized on the car's behalf, in the car's voice, a blue Volvo she had named Victoria (Victoria the first, I was the second). Who's to say what's even an accident? Who's to say there's a right way to show grief? So tear out your hair, go balding. Change the calendar, take a car ride back in time, take the wrong car that's the right car. Why must one always outlive the other?

✳

I once thought that if I drove out to Thousand Oaks and stood in Alice Coltrane's ashram, I'd understand Transcendence. If I buried myself in the sacred soil there, metaphorizing myself into sedentary academic decay,

I would have a rich understanding of Transcendence, the transferrable and distributed self, its detachment and transformation into metaphorical objects, the dynamics of spectacle, extreme physical activity, the impossibilities of material and movement that can only be achieved in dislocation from one's normal context, deterioration, entropy, decay. Instead, what happened was the ashram went to ashes, ash-rammed once I arrived, engulfed in wildfire flames, filling my pores with sound clouds, spinning me out into space camp. The ashram experience finished off Transcendence for me and wiped me clean, decamping and leaving me voided.

I don't remember how I got home that day.

✳

I was always reprimanded for asking the *world's most impossible questions* at dinnertime as a child and often that inner child continues to be reprimanded by the world. I'm forever opening a window and they're forever closing it, an inner world closing in on my inner child. I knew a former martial artist who became his own babysitter and would rock himself to sleep.

✳

What do you think this is "about?"

MADELINE

look, people are flawed and have limitations, and asking someone to change who they are, to simply undo these limitations, is not only hurtful but also a complete exercise in utter futility. my doc is always saying that i either need to accept the people in my life, limitations and all, or decide that the limitations are too annoying and end the relationships. most of the people in my life have mental problems, or at the very least, are terribly strange, and some of the strangeness is really irritating or even hurtful. but still that doesn't stop them from being loving, empathic human beings. if anything, i've noticed that the people in my life who have suffered the most are often the kindest and most understanding. and besides i also have my fair share of mental problems. so i need to either accept myself and my limitations or end the relationship with myself. which is an intriguing proposition.

i say this because something has been weighing on my mind, and i don't like myself for it. i was supposed to have an actual date on saturday, not a date where you sit around watching the marx brothers and then fuck, but a date *with DORA* that most likely would have involved being given flowers, then taken to the top of mulholland to watch the stars in the least scientific way possible, then going to some sort of tempeh dinner, but instead i had such panic and terror at the thought, that i made up some half-bullshit excuse about feeling too unwell and canceled. what in the fuck is wrong with me?! i have become one of those annoying, moody people who is destined to find misery at every turn. a snarky, miserable person who prefers her own strange company to real company.

oh, ouch. my high horse just trampled on me a bit as he rode away.

VICTORIA

I dream we're in a Lincoln town car careening along Mulholland. The driver cursed, though not maliciously exactly. We, the other three passengers, a young blonde pregnant girl with an orchid in her hair, William who was wearing soccer clothing and cleats, and myself, listened intently as the car careered around bend after bend. It's common for divers to curse, and in fact, most of America operates on this principle. But this driver wasn't cursing at another driver out of road rage at he who made a wrong turn, taking a hairpin turn at 50mph, fender-bending with a telephone pole, or even at God for giving him buckteeth and a potential lifespan of 48, but rather he was addressing a woman who wasn't there, a woman he was calling You Fucking Therapist. *Move out of the way, You Fucking Therapist!* he was yelling, *I need to get over!* and more ominously, *Get your goddamn ghost wagon off the road before you kill someone!*

The three of us moved back and forth in the vehicle in an endless nightmare like being stuck at the top of a roller coaster in the '80s with bad hair and no Gatorade. Like being in a haunted house where you give them your ticket to enter but can never exit and you have amnesia so every time a witch spits up to frighten you, it's like the first time, like an endless cycle of demonic possession. Madeline *found a way out*, he said, obviously thinking of another girl, *I wonder which door she went through*.

MADELINE

i've started writing little monologues (or sometimes dia-
logues, but where this one character is doing the bulk of the
talking, or the one character is doing *all* of the talking but
playing the role of both characters) on existential hopeless-
ness, depression, death, suicide, etc. but with the intent
of pointing out the humor in the level of self-absorption
and just general pomposity that often accompanies feeling that way. the sadness is very real but i couldn't help
but find a certain sick humor in the fact that i have once
again cut myself off from the world and all of it appears
to be catalyzed by a piece of "literary art." the fact that i
am using the "theater of the absurd" to validate my own
self-loathing and as an excuse to feel sorry for myself
while people are suffering around the world in all kinds
of hostile environments without any knowledge of beckett does seem, at the very least, a bit of my own theater
of the absurd. anyway i've been writing all of these little
monologues spoken by this character that's essentially an
exaggerated version of myself, exploring masculine and
feminine sides, my "bisexuality," and then suddenly i had
an idea for a play about a brother and sister, animus and
anima, who both are very depressed or believe themselves
to be very depressed and who are involved in the constant
struggle of keeping each other from self-harm while at
the same time trying to "out miserable" each other, both
believing that their own unique suffering is far worse than
the other's. which all leads back of course to *endgame* and
nell's "there is nothing quite so funny as unhappiness."

i tell my brother about this and he writes me:

> We need to make something about FW Murnau's head
> being stolen out of the family plot! insane!
> Sunrise is a really beautiful movie.
> Murnau was actually very handsome. I think he was
> queer.
> candle wax was found in the crypt or something. Are
> people that hellbent on accruing negative karma?
> He's been dead forever!
> He didn't even make a fucking talkie, he's been dead
> for so long!
> guess grave robbing is like bank robberies, people still
> do it, and even manage to not get caught.
> Well, they have the Venus-Saturn trine on their side,
> if anything. adds stability.
> Saturn rules prisons btw.

i don't know what to say about fw murnau's head being stolen other than it seems he's not the only one missing a head these days. yet despite my mental suffering which has taken on literary dimensions, i do think that being in love is a way out. and i think that maybe my feelings are building toward something important, which is to say, the real deal: the kind of affection that includes respect and a deep, indescribable human connection. you know, the kind of thing i've always thought was the stuff of legends and exaggeration and wishful thinking. and wuthering heights.

but that doesn't mean i can get out of the bathroom right now. i'm sorry, heathcliff, but momma needs to sit—or stay curled in a ball on the floor using the bath-mat as a blanket. i write dora the bad news that i need to reschedule our date due to "literary issues" and "acne" and "mold poisoning" and "pimple popping gone awry." she responds with a picture of ophelia drowning. i'm not sure if it's supposed to be me or her.

VICTORIA

I spent yesterday and last night traversing the Valley and watching the zombies vape for the first time. On Mulholland, I passed the pipe to the person in the back-seat before turning back to the wheel and crashing into a telephone pole. I guess I was trying to find some great patterns or design some new errors to correct the original errors. Trying to believe that in spite of or because of these imperfections life is worth living, only to realize that I am dead and somewhere in the dead world I am alive. And that not only am I not the author of my own existence but that the author of this entire situation is batshit fucking crazy. Sometimes I think I have a special bespoke key or am a special bespoke key and that despite all this chaos I continue unlocking truth, the same way chickweed climbs up out of grave plots. In any case, I have come to the conclusion that I am essentially not real, not unlike the shoplifted skinny jeans Sasha cut off me when she pulled me out of the wreckage.

MADELINE

*i am still homeless and "no pants." the cabaret singers
are to blame as are the gaping lapd and the hollywood
heartthrobs of 1999 and, apparently, ian mckellan, the
british homosexual. the valley has become a nice respite
for me in my homelessness "for rent," so i am grateful to
the fake residents and the nice furniture stores and con-
venient whole foods down the street. find me to follow
through with my laundry list of "assistance need" requests,
murder house help, time machine advice, some rehab for
sexual and spiritual abuse, armageddon talks, a new con-
federacy, and a good old time (for me, of course, since i
have been paralyzed since 5 years before). i am needed
in my local and abroad as a remote shamanic servant,
alchemist, bon vivant, and socialite "like my mom."
please put cash in my hand and get me an address. i do
not want to do time for "stealing diet coke." also, cabaret
people, i know you are trying to kill me with the lie that
my abusive 10 year vegetablization is a "culture" even
though it is still your job to be the middlemen and clean
the above-mentioned mess up fully at this point. one of
your bald ones tried to throw me out a window that was
a gaping hole with no railings. when i caught my breath
i made bees for the door and he snarked on me. all i did
was try to deliver the key*

that was the last thing i wrote before i lost my mind,
shaved off my eyebrows, took a bunch of vicodin, and
botched my suicide attempt. i showed it to dora: "i'd like
to take your sadness away."

VICTORIA

In the back of Sasha's car on the way to the hospital, I'm thinking of the tiny film I made of William in the desert, when our relationship was joined by the sleeves of our dead-punk shirts, sleeves that would later be emptied of their arms, arms disappearing into the landscape like the sun. How shall I show my grief? Tear out my hair, go bald like the moon. Suffer blow after blow on my conscious, deaden my mind, allow the smog to cloud my circuitry, my head swaying like hairballs in the wind, some landscape that knows no hair, has no memory strands, bad dye jobs, become timeless like mom, or let time move us when we're unmovable. I said the dumbest shit to my brother, cut his words on a lame bias just to make a point about bias, and now we're all balding, and I'm left with exposed remorse, have to cover all the mirrors with velvet drapes to glamorize my shame.

Only the image remains.

MAD

I find myself in a corner booth at DeMorgue's Pancake House on Ventura at 2 am, jacked up on prednisone, barely myself. My coherence abandoned itself years ago and its remnants are stale sugar crumbs in the greasy donut case.

Still, the donuts look delicious under-lit from across the room near the unmanned cash register. A mural on the wall shows giant utensils and sprinkled crullers and a teeny-tiny open coffin. The place smells like damp soil, more graveyard than restaurant, and the air is thick with dust particles, maybe ash. It's familiar. I used to come here all the time before I was whoever I am now, back when I was just a chubby kid making love to a stack of pancakes.

The waitress peeks out through the swinging door leading to the kitchen, chewing an unlit cigarette in the direction of her lone customer: me. I sit hunched, my hands slack on the sticky tabletop where the trace elements of strawberry jam meet with a forgotten trail of pancake sludge.

After awkward minutes (hours?) of avoiding direct eye contact, the waitress spits out her chewed-up cig and enters the landscape as though she's anticipating a dark future ahead of her: me.

"Diana" comes up to me, her name in quotes on the name tag. We're all in quotes in the Valley.

I order five cups of coffee to appear professional. She writes the word "coffee" down five times, then counts them. She asks if I want cream or sugar. I tell her I want both. She writes that down. "Can I see what you wrote?"

She cocks her head to one side. "You don't really want to know, do you?"

I shake my head no. Even though I do.

She disappears into a darkened carved-out space in the wall.

I stare at the CPR instructions sign above me, wondering if I could ever learn to resuscitate anything. Then I hear a voice.

✳

"I'm working on a novel about the Valley called *The San Fernando Valley.*" The voice is owned by a small, pale, bony, pretty birdlike girl, with innately intelligent eyes that are small and piercing and sad. She has wild Santa Ana windswept hair, the kind of ombre you might want to drink in the afternoon. There's an untouched stack of pancakes in front of her and she's wearing a ripped GG Allin "Legalize Murder" T-shirt.

"Not that you should care one bit about that," she smiles, "but you look like you're trying to write something, too. If only in your head."

"Yeah, I'm trying to write a book about the San Fernando Valley called *The Valley,*" I yell and feel very embarrassed about saying it out loud. "I'm failing miserably. Not to be confused with failing joyously." She takes her coffee mug and grabs her fur coat, crosses the Rubicon, and takes a seat across from me. "Have you tried writing exercises? A chiropractor? Visiting the grave of Chico Marx? The last one helped me a great deal."

"I have literary PTSD. I've tried everything, even

tearing pages off old copies of *Mad Magazine* and pitching them into the Valley's desert winds, only to have them rush back and cling to my face, leaving me shivering and in tears. I tried the same thing with Shirley MacLaine's autobiography and even Didion. The effect was the same, though, with *The White Album*, the pages refused to cling to any body part, preferring the company of a nearby concrete lamp post."

"That sounds difficult. Especially the bit about Didion."

"I just need the living to stop haunting me," I say. "And now that they're dead I really need them to leave me alone."

"The dead are terribly annoying. But for us loners and losers who feel alienated by this century, they're all we got."

"What's your name? I feel like I should know it already. Let me guess. Ophelia?"

She shakes her head.

"Constantine?"

She shakes her head.

"Dreidel?"

"Let me stop you. You look like you're in pain. My name's Mad. It's short for Madeline as in the sick French girl but also madness, as in its original meaning. Or Mutually Assured Destruction. Depends on who's asking."

"I'm Victoria. It's a name synonymous with victory. They thought I was going to be an athletic boy. Poor things."

Diana comes and wordlessly plops down five cups of coffee, a carafe of milk, and a ramekin filled with sugar.

Also, a lone coconut donut sitting on a plate.

"On the house," Diana says to the donut. "Anything more for you, honey?" she asks Mad.

"I suppose you don't have anything that will stop me from listening to Will Oldham albums and crying into a stuffed animal?"

"Not on the menu tonight."

"I'll just drink one of her cups, thank you."

Diana smiles at Mad, scowls at me, and floats back into the wall.

"So, writing," Mad says. "We can talk about it if you want. Happy to give you a reality check against a bad inner monologue."

"All I know is that when they find me dead, they'll find my notes on this work I've been chipping away at for my entire life. And it will only be comprised of thirteen unintelligible pages."

"Okay, never mind. You're fucked. Who is *they*?"

I can't answer because I can't remember.

"I get it," Mad says. "I'm massively depressed, occasionally manic, and often numb. I've been on and off mood stabilizers for the last week. I don't think I'm supposed to tamper with them like that. I just want people to like me, and I don't want to feel so sad all the time."

"At least you feel something. I can't even feel my legs anymore."

"Have you tried moving them?"

I look down and realize I've been sitting in a lotus position the entire time, which happens sometimes when I'm back in Southern California. I uncross my legs and feel needles shooting up and down them.

"Wait, why are you massively depressed?" I ask.

"Well, today marks the anniversary since my last breakdown and failed suicide thingy. I decided to honor the occasion by cleaning out the trunk of my car. I'd been avoiding it for over a year. But real adults clean the trunks of their automobiles. Honestly, I felt like burying a dead body. I took a Xanax, put on my headphones, and played Freddie Mercury's "Mr. Bad Guy" as loud as possible. I threw everything away except for this GG Allin T-shirt and my grandmother's chinchilla coat. At first, I took great comfort in knowing that it was basically all gone. But now, I feel bad for burying a dead body."

✳

I drink from the third cup of coffee and feel wetness on my cheek. Teardrops run down the windshields of my eyeglasses and heat fogs up the lens. Grief is embarrasing.

"Do you ever think about the time celebrity Valley twin Mary Kate Olsen was asked what happens when she's mistaken for her twin sister, Ashley?" I ask Mad.

"Rarely. But go on."

"Well, she said the difference to her was obvious: whereas Ashley thinks the opposite of fire is water to Mary Kate, the opposite of fire is no fire. This is the classic emotional crisis of seeing a two-face god, wondering which face is genuine and which is a piece of shit."

"So, are you Mary-Kate, Ashley, or The Vessel?" Mad asks me.

"I think when it comes to the Olsens, we're all the things, all the times."

Mad gets a faraway look in her eye. She dunks a partially consumed coconut donut in one of my cups of coffee, then carefully places it on her tongue. Feeling vulnerable, I am suddenly aware of the growing bald spot at the back of my head exposed to the A/C blasting from the ceiling.

"I've been chipping away my novel," she says. "But I think I'm doing it all wrong."

"In what sense? Like bit by bit?"

"No, I've been chipping it like a pet cat is chipped. I follow the chipped pet, my unwritten novel, around, hoping the cat will lead me to some epiphany. Every time, I end up in the gutter licking shrimp shells."

She crop-circles her finger around a donut's crumb. "Yes, solitude has always driven me to the brink. It was initially creatively useful but now seems to be a punishment. Every day, I can't go on. But I go on anyway. It's terribly boring."

"But it's *our* boring," I say as I smile, a little too enthusiastically.

She looks at me as she thoughtfully places the crumb in her mouth.

✳

"I grew up in what's known as the Narcissistic Family Complex," she tells me. "My father was a closeted gay. Though when one looks back at images, it's hard to understand the 'closeted' part, considering his penchant for Liberace, Versace, la Cucaracha."

I'm turned on.

"One time my father made them throw a birthday party for him and print out images of his favorite celebrities—

Elizabeth Taylor, Vanessa Redgrave, all the Pointer Sisters—and string them around the house in vibrant Kodachrome, reverse-processed to aesthetic highs, an image bursting out of its cells.

"My brother and I also had to come up with a signature drink for the deranged affair, which ended up being called Pink Daddy. By the end of the night, many of the partygoers were hanging on a fringed chandelier, an undulating celestial body, as I read aloud to the group the poem I had written for my dad, 'Elegy for a Frog.' The guests quickly started calling it 'Elegy for a Fag.' When our mother came to pick us up she found us passed out in a corner surrounded by bits of magenta taffeta."

"Oh, my god. How old were you?" I ask.

"Seven."

I feel like I'm looking through a window into a mirror, a body shadowed into the background, a body without a head.

"He left for Italy," Mad says. "And soon thereafter began parasitically attaching himself to older gentlemen. He recently popped up on documentary television as an interview subject about gay ex-pats living in Puglia. That was the last time I saw him.

"I tried killing him in my dreams but turns out it's impossible. At the same time, all creation is the work of God, even the depraved, because men are frail, pathetic, fragile, dumb reeds bending against the great wild storm, crying alone in shallow puddles. So, I made him human and never looked back."

"Is this person deranged?" I can't tell if I am asking

about Mad or her Pink Daddy or myself. The sugar is getting to my head, and I suddenly need a massive brick of protein. I ask Mad how to get to the Valley Store from here, the one with a butcher that sells veal chops, next to the donut store Holly's, not too far from the Brady Bunch House but not too close either, you know the one.

"Um, I'm not really sure. I thought we were in Iowa City."

"Dear God! I thought I was in Los Angeles!"

But we *are* in Los Angeles, or some version of it, the Midwest version of it, the Valley.

Just then, the lights go out in my head. But just before I notice Diana standing over me with a broken coffee pot.

✳

When I come to, we are in a limousine on Mulholland Drive.

Mad and I are in the backseat and I'm still unable to tell where the dream ends and reality begins, where Mad is and I'm not. As one, we are the Head of the Nocturnal Society, ruled not by cynicism but by metaphysical proclamations, a reversal of the tenets of atheism, a place where *dog* is *God* spelled backward. The diner coffee was surely drugged.

Suddenly, the limo is speeding out of its lane and crashes into a mailbox. We exit the limo at the crash site, which happens to be Mad's house. The driver is nowhere to be found if there ever was a driver in the first place. I pick up the mail and look through it like a detective. Every envelope is stamped with a different year.

Mad takes me by the elbow into the hot night air, scissored moonlight fissuring the sky. She picks up a fallen partially burned palm frond and begins fanning me with it.

"You walk with the kind of trepidation that some lunatics display." She seems to know what she's talking about. Someone has said that to her before.

❋

We enter Mad's neglected succulent garden.

There's a miniature grotto, a slumbering rattlesnake, and a record player spinning Silence. Staring at the chlorinated water, I think women should beware of wandering alone at night. A shallow pool can be an ocean if we drown. Mad looks at me in agony.

"You know, things used to be so simple. I'd get home after a long day, brush my teeth, smoke some pot, pick up the heaping mound of clothes on my floor, and ruminate first," she says to me. "Now I ruminate last. The world's gone mad."

Her house is blurry, the lighting dim. I feel disoriented and mid-stroke-like. Among the other many torturous knickknacks in the living room are an imposing fake fig tree, a giant abacus, and a recent edition of the *DSM* torn to bits. In a corner sits a blindfolded bust of Saint Judas with a flame around his head. On the wall is a dilapidated taxidermized squirrel.

"Oh, I've been meaning to repair that," Mad says to the squirrel.

There is a vintage Prozac sign that must have once been hung in a psychiatrist's office. A paperweight from the Iowa State Fair in the shape of a pregnant hog sits on a table. But the weirdest is a garish *objet d'art* placed on a marble slab dead center in the room: a life-size Grecian cremation urn.

"Oh, that houses the cremains of my father, who isn't dead. It's just cigarette butts I had blessed by a Rabbi. My dad's Catholic."

I stare at the inanimate object, marveling at how an object doesn't have genitals, an identity, an orientation, or a desire. How happy a pot must be. "Do you ever get sad on Father's Day?"

"Yeah, I usually have issues on Father's Day. I tend to opt for a day's worth of drug-induced sleep. This past Father's Day I went to Balboa Park to throw stones at the geese and make nasal sounds. I fell asleep on a little island in the middle of the pond away from the human traffic. I awoke hungrily just before sundown and thought about maybe trying to jack off before heading home. Suddenly, my phone rang. It was a guy I used to be friends with who essentially molested me on Father's Day a few years ago. At first, I thought 'What in the actual fuck?' and then 'That's a make-out session I definitely don't want' and then curiously, I hoped he would leave a message and tell me I was the hottest teenager he had ever tried to get with. Well, he did leave a message and I guess he thought that after sexually violating me and not speaking to me for a few years, he'd call me up on a Saturday night and invite me to a Catholic mass the next day. Yes, church. It's a straaaange worrrrld," Mad drawls.

We both stare at the Angel of Death hanging from her crystal chandelier. I take my hand in hers.

✳

Mad grabs a compass sitting at the feet of the Grecian urn to guide us into her bedroom. It happens to be decorated exactly as my own teenage bedroom was: posters of homosexual porn stars from the '80s, wax candles in the shape of tits, pillows without pillowcases, a black comforter screaming depression, a dish of broken jeans zippers, a framed picture of my mom in a belted leotard teaching high-impact aerobics.

Not a lot is reaching the surface of consciousness this evening but one thing is certain: I feel like my breasts are missing. A lot is missing. I clutch my thinning ponytail. I literally kick myself for allowing sorrow and anxiety to arise just when I am enjoying myself.

"I don't mean to be weird, but do you believe in nervous breakdowns?"

Mad grabs my leg and stops me from kicking myself.

"Medically speaking there is no such thing as a nervous breakdown. It's just a pop culture term for 'going batshit' that sounds more formal. Honestly, if you want to know about nervous breakdowns, I'd recommend you go listen to Sid Vicious."

I know I've heard this before.

Mad gets me a blonde wig to match the color of her hair. She brings me up to a large mirror, puts our heads together, and breathes words onto the mirror: "You look more like yourself."

"Sorry, in the absence of medical personnel, I need to splash water on my face to make sure I'm okay."

I go to the bathroom and shut the door. On a drawing hung over the toilet is an imagined wake for Russell Brand, two versions of his soul splitting off, one that looks like Katy Perry and one that looks like Kate Moss.

Across it is a thought-bubble reading, "My life is essentially a series of embarrassing incidents strung together by me telling people about those embarrassing incidents."

I splash water across my face and try to wash my anxiety away with a Lexapro-logo hand towel.

*

Back in the bedroom is a worn-out stripper pole that seems to have traveled a great distance.

"My ex put one of those in our garage," I say. I want to tell Mad how Dora liked Winona Ryder and stripping and sometimes both at the same time, but then remember talking about an ex is a dreadful way to get to know someone.

Mad goes to our bedside table drawer and pulls out a picture. "I have a Dora myself."

It's an image of a woman working a pole in San Francisco, surrounded by drag queens and wearing a little hat that says, MAYOR. "The queens deputized her. They were, how do you say, totally knackered. She says one day I can be her deputy mayor. She's fun. I think we need people like this in our lives, you and me. To get us out of our Beckett inertia." Mad tosses the photo back into the drawer.

She grabs my hand and we both take turns twirling around the pole, Mad like an elegant carousel and me like the awkward fireman, reminding me of all my problems with time, gravity, circumlocution, pornography's constellation.

"When did you move into my bedroom?" I ask.

"It was after you moved to Iowa. I've moved 27 times

in my life, but I always return here for a bad time."

My wig goes crooked.

✳

The bed seems to have chunky blood on it.

"If I get any more chipotle salsa on my bed sheets, just start calling me fatty," Mad says. "I know, I weigh, like 90 pounds, but sometimes obesity is less about the look and more about the lifestyle. Nothing says 'I've given up on sex' like sauce-stained bedsheets. I hope you won't hold it against me."

"Look, when I was your age I used to think love was a comforter. But now I wonder if it's not more like hitting myself in the face with a pillowcase filled with nails. Over and over again. Sorry, that was foreplay."

"I like it," Mad says. "Very Catholic."

I unbutton my blouse, she unzips her pants. I remove my socks, she teases off my bra. I rip off my jeans, she removes her Band-Aids.

I plop down on a beanbag chair, my old beanbag chair. "I used to sing along to Elliot Smith on this cushion." It was in this room I first learned that reality was more romantic than dreams.

Mad says, "Sorry, it's hard to take you seriously with your tits out."

I look down at my socks and underwear but somehow can't bear to take them off. "I was much more fun before I went to art school."

Mad takes off her top and tosses it into a corner. "Look, I'm not sure it does much good to cultivate a detached sensibility by being angry and irreverent all the time. Don't get too down on yourself. It's a dog's life for the modern American artist." Mad pets a stuffed animal bunny.

"Yeah," I say, "I just get sad sometimes thinking about Mom."

"Maybe the poor woman is just tired and ready to go and you have to accept that." Mad lights a joint, inhales, and passes it to me. "She's like fucking Rasputin. There comes a point where you just think: 'I want peace.'"

"Just promise me one day you'll demand the respect you deserve," I say as I inhale deeply. "I never really learned."

Mad nods. "Yeah, I used to attract shitty lovers as a kind of hobby, letting myself be treated like shit as long as I was getting attention. It wasn't an especially good look. But the other night this thing happened. Keep in mind I was very stoned and wearing short-shorts. Anyway, I said to Dora, my current crush, 'I'm the kind of girl you only get one chance with. Don't blow it.' I have no idea why I said it. Maybe she looks like someone who could break my heart."

I'm suddenly very stoned. "Are all Doras sexy mental patients? Once I tried to stick up for myself when we were listening to a podcast about narcissistic abuse. She asked if I wanted to make out."

"That's kinda hot," Mad says. "Did you?"

"Of course. Both my brother and I have a knack for attracting some riffraff. Hm 'had.' I can't keep the tenses straight. I remember when I first heard about my brother dying, or I guess his suicide thingy, or whatever happened, there was this intense feeling of my body separating from my mind. I'm not saying it's all related to Dora or Doras.

But it might be. I think about my epitaph all the time now."

We lie in silence, side by side, with the stuffed animal bunny between us.

I relax into her body and say. "I feel so strange, like an image that keeps getting reprinted. I'm stuck in a Morrissey loop."

"I once read on the internet that friends don't let friends listen to The Smiths when they are depressed. I mean, fucking hell, take these records away from us!"

I sit up, very very stoned, since I'm used to '90s weed. I say to Mad: "I think I'm in love with you."

"Have you done this before?" Mad asks.

"What?" I ask back.

Mad nods.

"I'm not sure."

✳

I have two faces, one turned toward the world and one turned against it, the essential qualities of lightness and darkness, brother and sister, male and female.

Mad adds more hair to me where there is balding and sadness. She put a little mustache over my mouth so I can't talk. She rocks me back and forth, which seems like the wrong configuration, so then I begin to rock her, soothing her, cooing.

Suddenly, I find myself being pleasantly smothered with a down pillow over my face, Mad pressing into me as we move from abyss to void to outer space. Her chinchilla fur is thrown over the beanbag chair, her GG Allin shirt is torn to tattered bits as are my jeans from clawing at each other. We're punching, kicking, and biting.

Then Mad taps her forehead into the wall and shakes with exasperation as she yells, "Victoria, you're a guy!"

✳

Illumination of nights, orbits of visions, my eternal orb, my baldness. Or is that the moon coming in through the bedroom window? I hear a shrieking seagull. And suddenly, my mustache drops off, my eyes are where my knees should be, then Mad's eyes are on my forehead looking out. Drops of dew on my forehead. Mad moves her arms like branches, her mouth fills with foam. Her body casts a shadow over mine like a sail. Waves begin to rise.

There is no better test of love than rough experience.

I quickly shave off Mad's eyebrows, like the Mona Lisa, adding beauty to her face. She rips off the hair weave that was covering up my bald spot and tosses it on the ground.

My head gongs like a bell when Mad raps me over the head with my childhood copy of *Grey's Anatomy*. I smack her bare knee with the pink clarinet from my childhood. We're both fighting phantoms with surfaces that appear only to disappear.

What happened? What's going to happen?

"In the present tense, please!" Mad pleads.

She kisses me hard. Then she enters me, her head almost fully in the back of my mouth.

Mad breaks free from the edge of oblivion. "I love you! Don't ever forget me!" Mad yells as she slaps me across the face, the same place where Diana the waitress hit me with the coffee pot years before.

I stare at the claw-shaped print of my hand across Mad's forehead. I swoon and pass out onto the beanbag chair.

We both sleep, interlocked, unaware of the scrutiny. One of her breasts had been carved into, a botched amputation, a homemade tattoo. The breast is mine.

"*The Valley*!" we awake and scream out loud.

VICTORIA

At some point, I guess Will lost his skylight, no stars, just full-on darkness.

✳

He spent most of his days writing his Living Will, fumbling through words with his stiffening fingers, willing his will to live, every so often changing the instructions for the undertaker. He insisted on being buried at sea in a Pride flag though he was neither gay nor prideful. He asked for his membership to the Insect Society be canceled, that his diploma certificate as a Graduate of the School of Flesh be turned into compost. He asked that it be arranged for someone to leave a seagull egg and a bottle of pasteurized strawberry milk at his mother's doorstep until further notice and for many years beyond. He asked to donate his vintage entombed butterfly named Sofia to the Natural History Museum. And to notify the postman of his address change from his mother's house to his mother's backyard, c/o Fairy Grotto.

✳

Back at Skyla's, I sit down in Will's ergonomic chair to look through his desk for the will and noted the framed photographs—one of Crystal and Mash on party donkeys in Mexico, one of me fully covered in a black tarp in Last Chance, Iowa's non-perpetual care cemetery, one of Sasha and him holding a ukulele on an overcast beach and finally the original photo of which I had a copy, of my brother at a dude ranch. I have a moment of respect for my brother, that the one good thing my brother did was kill himself before the Dark Ages were full upon us, before society had gone into full-force goblin mode, engulfing himself in a sea of brightness before the dark.

I open the drawer and come across a letter he wrote me, but never sent.

hey mad,
it's a weirdly stormy evening, the first in ages, and you're locked away. the world might be ending. i've been thinking about what i want to say to you if it does. somehow tonight in my own mixed up internal world, i have come to associate our lost connection with the dramatic and tragic split of oasis—did you know they were originally called 'the rain'?—and all the reality and mythology surrounding noel and liam: one a deeply disturbed, chaotic and selfish nar-cissistic personality disorder. the other, an equally disturbed and chaotic man trying his best to hang on to his love for the other while simultaneously trying to keep his own internal demons at bay. the latter, a man who one day simply had enough and smashed his brother's guitar backstage over an argument about leather jackets.

one can only endure such drama for so long, and i have come to realize i have at times been liam to your noel, an unflattering comparison to say the least. so when the brothers both recently announced that they were going to bury the hatchet, i cried tears of joy! what a wonderful sentiment in conjunction with my own internal symbolism about our 'brotherhood' as you used to call it. today, as i discussed this with the therapist in my head, i wept into the emptiness: "this is not how it was meant to be. i need her and she needs me."

unlike oasis we have only our own feelings to wade through, no media circus, no cocaine binges, no tossing of tambourines, no pressure to produce a better album than our first. we have only ourselves. i know that we are human beings and not a brit rock band, and that rock n roll is dead. i know things can never be the way they were before, it can't always be like that day when we were teenagers and impulsively went to the desert on new year's and got our heads shaved and tried to make a film.

please know i'm sorry for the things i have done and the things i didn't do. seeing you sick has been too hard for me. it reminds me of things i hate in myself. instead of taking space i should have gotten closer. i'm not very strong i could say a million more things, but i'll leave this as it is. the storm of the century is flooding the garage and perhaps having a garage band was never a good idea anyway. but for what it's worth, i love you, mad, i really do.
- noel

My mom interrupts me, looking for me "to help steer." She exists now amongst the sequined fishes where the tide had washed over her. Underneath her is a red carpet made of starfish. She tells me about the indentations from surfers upon the silk pillows. About a lobster who wore pearls and a stone crab who broke all the mirrors. She pulls out of her pocket a pink feathered boa and wraps it around my neck as evidence of her adventures. Mom then turns and begins talking to a human-sized seagull.

I put my hand on her. "Mom, I'll always love you even though I've lost a part of you inside of me and maybe you've lost parts of yourself." She's silent, and I suddenly remember her botched mastectomy, and the Fairy tattoo she had gotten soon thereafter to cover the scar, some fairy dust reminding her to never give up on dreaming.

"I'm sorry this happened, that Will did this. That he went mad."

"Bullshit!" Mom exclaims. "Nonsense!"

"What's bullshit? What's nonsense?"

"Your brother didn't kill himself. He was an idiot! The cops said it was an accident. Eyewitnesses say he was filming himself monologuing. Monologuing! About what! Your brother wasn't crazy, he was a moron!"

We're both silent.

"I love you, whoever you are," Mom says to me as she floats back to wherever she was before.

✳

I grab my brother's car keys off his desk and sneak past mourners into the garage. I see Sasha sitting behind the wheel of the car. She doesn't look at me as I open the door and get in the passenger seat. She's listening to synth-heavy classical music, like from an '80s film that doesn't exist. I remember suddenly that when Will and I got our licenses, we would each take the Saab up to Mulholland and drive its length. I always hoped someone would see me behind the wheel with my sunglasses on even at night and think: "*Who* is that lesbian in an old car?" But I don't think anyone ever noticed me.

Sasha looks at me. She smiles and says: "It's the soundtrack Will made to your film. He was working on it for the past year. He was making new music and editing scenes. The one you guys originally shot in the desert. Where he's playing Lucifer and you're playing a schizophrenic lesbian ethnographer studying demonic possession. It looked really cool."

I didn't know he made a soundtrack to the film we never made. It's actually quite good, like some weird by-product of sleep deprivation and too many synthesizers.

Sasha turns down the music slightly so that it's background noise, our soundtrack in this moment. She grabs her phone, pulls up a video, and hits Play. On the screen is a scene I shot for the film out in Yucca Valley, on the day of a solar eclipse. In it, my brother, high on Ritalin and dressed demonically, gets up on a boulder. He's holding a 35mm camera and begins to dumbly shoot it like a pistol. As the sun becomes obscured by the moon, he improvises dialogue, yelling gleefully into the landscape: "We'll hang ourselves tomorrow... unless Godot comes!" You can hear me call back from behind the camera, "And if he comes?" My brother smiles and throws his arms into the air, screaming at the universe: "Then we'll be saved!" The camera lingers on him as the landscape and everything in it takes on a metallic hue and then goes darker.

The video ends. We're silent for a moment. Then Sasha says, "I really love your family, but sometimes I think: it shouldn't be so hard to be normal."

I choke back tears but also laugh a little, "It is if you're nuts. It's the hardest thing." I look at her.

"I loved your brother," she says, and I can see it's true.

"Wanna take a ride somewhere?" she asks. I think for a minute. "Just for a little bit. We can't really go that far anyway. The Valley is everywhere."

We make the kind of eye contact you make when you're about to fall in love or already have. Maybe I just miss him, maybe this is how I can get closer. "Let's take a drive," I nod.

She revs the engine and pulls out of Skyla's compound. We head along Mulholland toward the Pacific Ocean, perhaps hoping that the tides will return some of what the tides took out of us.

As we snake away, I watch as the Santa Ana winds stir up dust in the Valley basin as wildfires crest towards my mother's house, the long swells of flames consuming the empty and echoing rooms, the flames billowing over the roof, melting the already peeling cornices, the shattered widows and the broken mirrors, destroying the very firmament of the universe, the Fairy Grotto and my mother's dreams, turning all that had been into nothing.

I pull down the sun visor and look in the mirror. I notice soft blonde baby hairs growing back around my scalp line. Behind me, the Valley ashes and deserts itself. I feel around in my pockets for a dissociative, finger it, but think better.

THE VALLEY a void
by Vanessa Roveto

Co-Publishers: Bruno Ceschel, Nicholas Muellner
and Catherine Taylor
Designer: Brian Paul Lamotte
Editors: Catherine Taylor and Nicholas Muellner
Proofreader: Erin Adamo
Project Manager: Hannah Dunsmore
Typeface: Untitled Sans and Untitled Serif
Printer: Grafiche Veneziane
Printed and bound in Italy

First edition published in September 2023
by SPBH Editions and ITI Press

SPBH Editions is the publishing house of
Self Publish Be Happy Ltd., Studio 2,
38-50 Pritchard's Rd, London E2 9AP, UK
www.selfpublishbehappy.com

ITI Press is affiliated with the Image Text MFA
at Cornell University, College of Architecture Art & Planning
www.imagetextithaca.com

Vanessa Roveto would like to thank ITI Press and SPBH Editions,
and especially Nicholas Muellner and Catherine Taylor for making
this book possible. To my early readers, Tom and Nick, for their
thoughtful feedback. To my mother, always. And to Anna, my
sharper eye, for traveling with me to the Valley and beyond.

ISBN 9781739606749